THIS TOUCHING, PASSIONATE NOVEL OF SELF-
DISCOVERY AND SEXUAL AWAKENING "MAY
WELL TURN OUT TO BE A CLASSIC."
> —Russell Banks, author of *Continental Drift*

"This is some of the brightest, funniest, most touching
writing about adolescence I've read in a long time. And
if ever a book will give straight readers an exact sense of
what it's like to grow up gay, surely *The Boys on the Rock*
will. We've had novels about gays who are elegant, artistic,
alienated; how great to have one at last about the regular,
popular, handsome, athletic guy who just happens to be
. . . well, you know . . . a little weird."
> —Edmund White, author of *A Boy's Own Story*

"John Fox is a young talented writer with a singular voice.
The Boys on the Rock is a unique coming-of-age novel. It
is filled with wit . . . and fleshed out with characters rarely
encountered in contemporary fiction."
> —Richard Price, author of *The Breaks*

JOHN FOX is from the Bronx and lives in Manhattan.
His fiction appeared for the first time in *Christopher
Street,* and he is now working on a second novel.

THE BOYS ON THE ROCK

JOHN FOX

A PLUME BOOK

NEW AMERICAN LIBRARY

NEW YORK AND SCARBOROUGH, ONTARIO

PUBLISHERS NOTE

This novel is a work of fiction. Names, characters, places, and incidents either are the product of the author's imagination or are used fictitiously, and any resemblance to actual persons, living or dead, events, or locales is entirely coincidental.

NAL BOOKS ARE AVAILABLE AT QUANTITY DISCOUNTS WHEN USED TO PROMOTE PRODUCTS OR SERVICES. FOR INFORMATION PLEASE WRITE TO PREMIUM MARKETING DIVISION, NEW AMERICAN LIBRARY, 1633 BROADWAY, NEW YORK, NEW YORK 10019.

This is an authorized reprint of a hardcover edition published by St. Martin's Press.

Original hardcover design by Lee Wade

 PLUME TRADEMARK REG. U.S. PAT. OFF. AND FOREIGN COUNTRIES REG. TRADEMARK—MARCA REGISTRADA HECHO EN FAIRFIELD, PA., U.S.A.

SIGNET, SIGNET CLASSIC, MENTOR, PLUME, MERIDIAN AND NAL BOOKS are published *in the United States* by New American Library, 1633 Broadway, New York, New York 10019, *in Canada* by The New American Library of Canada Limited, 81 Mack Avenue, Scarborough, Ontario M1L 1M8

Library of Congress Cataloging in Publication Data

Fox, John, 1952-
   The boys on the rock.

   Summary: A sixteen-year-old from the Bronx, popular at school and "sort of" going steady, falls in love for the first time with another boy one exuberant summer.
   [1. Homosexuality—Fiction]   I. Title.
PS3556.O934B6   1985   813'.54   [Fic]   85-8795
ISBN 0-452-25753-0 (pbk.)

First Plume Printing, September, 1985

      3   4   5   6   7   8   9

PRINTED IN THE UNITED STATES OF AMERICA

To Russell Banks and Janet Chalmers

THE
BOYS
ON
THE
ROCK

ONE OF TOMMY'S LEGS IS SHORTER than the other and thin as a rail. He had polio as a child although how I know this or how anyone knows it I can't remember because it's something you never heard him talk about, and whenever anyone else talked about it they'd whisper as if he was five feet away even when he was nowhere around. He has this very square jaw with muscles on it that he'd flex and lock and unlock when he was embarrassed or angry about his leg, which was quite often, and he'd usually wind up taking it out on Lorraine, who has these huge tits that he's crazy about. She's very large and tall—almost as tall as I am, and whenever she took off her glasses to clean them she looked like she was looking in about five different directions at once—including you—but some people thought she was sort of pretty.

She *was* very bighearted. Like on account of Tommy's leg for example, she'd sell refreshments at Kathy's, the school she used to go to. Tommy would never dance because of his leg in other words, so you'd always see the two of them behind the refreshment counter tangled up on one folding chair with his head buried in her tits, and if you were thirsty or anything you could forget about it. Very few people ever bothered trying to get to know Tommy and they always wondered what the hell Lorraine saw in him because they thought he was such a turd.

The first Sunday in June—two and a half months ago, June '68— was his seventeenth birthday party in his backyard and there was a big crowd of our friends there as well as his relatives and various other people eating and drinking having a good time on this very muggy hazy day. We all got quite polluted and eventually Tommy and Lorraine, me, my friend Joey and his girlfriend Roxanne and some girl who I was supposedly sort of seeing named Sue decided to go to this place called the Neck Inn which is this bar with a rock band at the tip of Throgs Neck under the bridge where you can dance and drink and carry on and hang out. It's very easy to get in there even if you aren't eighteen. I'm sixteen. I have a fake draft card which they never once asked me for, not even the very first time we went there, maybe because I'm five eleven. Joey had his father's new used car, this boat, this Impala, so he drove, with Roxanne to his right who was all over him and next to her was this girl Sue who I was supposedly sort of going out with, looking straight ahead and behind her was me with my knees so close to my chin I could have reached them with my tongue practically, the seat was pushed back so far—in order for Joey's stomach to fit behind the steering wheel. He's very fat.

So Sue in front of me flips her hair over the back of the seat and it hangs down and dangles like four inches from my nose with Tommy and Lorraine going at it full force to my left, sweating with the two of them doing their "Ohh I love you" routine and Lorraine's hair swinging and flapping all over the place, like in my face.

The two of them had been going out together since around puberty and they got engaged when they were fourteen. No one I've ever met has gotten engaged that young and as far as I know neither one ever had sex with anyone but each other until this night of Tommy's party. You could tell they were constantly fucking and if you couldn't figure it out for yourself they'd let you know themselves if you hung around them often enough because they loved to talk about it and complain and argue about birth control pills and periods and Trojans and various things like that which kind of gross me out. You'd be in the middle of a conversation with them on the corner or on a bench in Pelham Bay Park or in the back seat of a car and they'd suddenly start making out real passionately and Tommy would immediately go for those tits and Lorraine would moan and toss her hair all over the place, like in your face, and say, "Ohh Tommy ohhh Tommy I love you I love you," and he'd come up for air every now and then and say things like, "Lorraine Lorraine I love you I love you," and then they'd start whispering and complaining and arguing about some very brilliant subject like the ones I just mentioned. Either they were making out wherever they happened to be or else they were arguing. One or the other.

It only took about fifteen minutes to get to the Neck Inn but by the time we did Tommy and Lorraine were into one of their fights and he was refusing to go inside. Joey went right in with Roxanne and I told this girl Sue she should go inside with them and we'd be right in. Tommy started limping across the dirt parking lot, kicking rocks, yelling things at Lorraine over his shoulder which you couldn't hear on account of the roar of the bridge overhead.

Whenever they argued he'd call her rotten untrue insulting names and she'd cry and run to me if I was around and I'd tell her not to cry because Tommy really loves her and he's just jealous because he has an inferiority complex and I know and she knows that he's really a hell of a sweet guy and then they'd meet halfway and make up. Later on Tommy would come over to me and we'd talk about everything and anything except him and Lorraine and you could tell he was grateful to me because whatever it was I said to Lorraine, which I knew he didn't want to hear, always got them back together again.

So I picked up my cue and went into my Tommy's-a-Great-Guy-He's-Just-Jealous routine with Lorraine and she stopped crying and went running after him, but he didn't turn around to meet her halfway like he usually did. I figured he'd get around to it in a minute so I went inside where Roxanne and Sue were dancing and Joey was hanging out at the bar with some guys we knew so I went over there and we were drinking and carrying on in the red dark light.

Tommy and Lorraine finally came in and they each bought a drink at the other end of the bar. I motioned for them to come on over by us but they didn't budge. A girl on a bar stool near Tommy got up and he sat down. Lorraine glanced at me. Actually she *snuck* a glance at me, and then she turned and looked at the back of Tommy's head. She was wolfing at her drink and every now and then she'd whisper something in his ear and he'd make some kind of flip gesture with the flat of his hand, the way you would if someone kept bothering the hell out of you while you were trying to concentrate on something real important and all he was doing was watching the bartender washing glasses and making drinks, getting change and taking jackets for people and stuffing them into these heavy wooden beams above the bar that are supposed to make the place look western or colonial or something. Lorraine tossed me another top-secret signal and I went over there and stood there. Tommy didn't even turn around. Our eyes met in the mirror and he looked down and tipped his drink to his mouth. Meanwhile, Lorraine's head is going back and forth between me and Tommy, her face all screwed up, like she was trying to decide.

Then to his shoulder Tommy said, "Why don't you go dance with Billy?" With Tommy you can't always tell if he's mad or what. The way he said that it sounded like a civil polite question.

I said, "Are you sure?" Then I felt pretty stupid. I mean, Lorraine had danced with me plenty of times before that without asking him if it was okay. He didn't say anything. So we went to dance. But it was a slow dance and she seemed to be making some kind of point to Tommy who was getting shitfaced, shaking his leg back and forth, glaring at us with his jaw muscles. Lorraine was grinding up against me, had me in a bear hug, I could hardly breathe and at the same time she's trying to hold on to her drink, spilling it on my back, so I said, "Uh, listen Lorraine, why don't you go over to Tommy? I don't want to dance anymore."

"I don't want to go anywhere near him," she says.

"Why not?"

"I don't like him anymore. I wish he would drop dead." She was sort of slurry-worded.

"Oh come on, you don't mean any of that."

"I do *too!*" and she pulled me tighter and sloshed some more of her screwdriver down my back so I shook her off and took her by the arms and said, "I don't think this was such a good idea, Lorraine. Why don't you go back over there before he ruptures a jaw muscle or something."

But she wouldn't go, so I went over to him and with his leg shaking like crazy and his jaw muscles flying all over the place he says, "You fucking traitor what the fuck are you grinding my girlfriend my fucking fian*cée* for all over the fucking dance floor."

"Look, I think you're both acting pretty weird," I said, "and I don't exactly appreciate being put in the middle of one of your dumb-ass fights."

So he flies off the bar stool at me, takes a swing at my face and loses his balance, regains it and I take a swing at him for some reason and he ducked and I missed. We were both quite drunk in other words. A bouncer came over and told us to cool it or he'd kick our asses out. Tommy gulped down his drink and left.

Joey and Roxanne didn't catch any of this because they were going at it in some corner and I couldn't find Lorraine or Sue anywhere and then Sue—this one who I was sort of seeing—came out of the ladies room and said that Lorraine was in there crying. I went to the bar and Sue followed me. I ordered my millionth beer of the day. Some guy asked Sue to dance and she looked at me and I took a slug of beer and she went with this guy to dance. He put his hands on her ass and pressed her into his crotch and he was sort of gnawing at her ears and face and she dropped her head back so he wouldn't miss her neck. Lorraine came out of the ladies room and over to me, sort of nuzzling up to me with her tits, saying she loves *me* not Tommy and she wants to make love to me and all this, and tears are all over her face and then out of nowhere I hear, "I hope I'm not breaking *up* anything." This was Sue with her hands on her hips and I swear she was tapping her foot. A rolling pin was all she needed. To my bottle of beer I said, "I want to get out of here," and I downed it. Lorraine and Sue at the same time said, "So do I," and they looked at each other.

Joey and Roxanne were still at it in some corner and they didn't exactly look like they were ready to leave but I went over to them anyway and asked Joey if he felt like driving us home and he mumbled "No" without taking his mouth off Roxanne's. So I called a cab.

The three of us got in with me in the middle. The cab driver's eyes through the rearview mirror wanted to know Where To, and Sue's address cáme out my mouth. She stiffened on my left and Lorraine relaxed on my right and we rode in complete silence and it took forever. When we got to Sue's she got out, slammed the cab door and ran straight inside. The screen door slammed, the stoop light went out and the next thing I remember is sort of wafting into Pelham Bay Park with Lorraine or me swigging at a 32-ounce bottle of Colt. It was sticky and the park was thick gray in the night.

Lorraine was talking a mile a minute about how inconsiderate Tommy was and he didn't satisfy her sexual desires and all this. We cleared some broken glass off some steps on Rice Stadium and sat down and she said, all slurry-worded, "Billy, you're so sexy and handsome. And so intelligent." She was sitting right next to me, leaning on me, holding my arm. I was watching moist yellow circles pulse around the lights, changing shape each time I blinked.

She started feeling up my thigh, stroking it, rubbing it. "You're so tall," she said. "You have such long legs." I took a slug of beer. She started licking my ear and I told her to quit it. She said, "But Billy, I love you, I *love* you."

"Oh, come on," I said, "you love Tommy." I moved her hand off my leg.

"Don't push me away."

I kept drinking the beer even though I was already very bombed. She put her hand back on my thigh and started rubbing my cock and I started to get a hard-on. The next thing I remember is being in the undeveloped part of the park where there's a huge grassy field which dips and slopes down to a stone wall that runs along the water. It was a very romantic setting in other words, with the lights on City Island sparkling and there were stars out twinkling and a moon bright through the haze and the huge chestnut tree down by the water stood still, blue in the light. Every now and then you'd hear a car on Watt Avenue, not far from my house.

We laid down in the grass and she started unbuckling my pants and I started unbuttoning her blouse and my hands started feeling up those tits that Tommy is so crazy about. We got our clothes sort of partially off and she straddled me and rode me like a cowgirl, her hair flying and she was crying and sometimes she'd say, "Ohh Billy ohhh Billy," which is my name, and sometimes she'd say, "Ohh Tommy ohhh Tommy" and sometimes she'd say "Ohh Tommy, I mean ohh Billy" and I wondered what Tommy saw in those huge tits. I stopped noticing the stars and the moon and kept spotting old pieces of newspaper and beer cans and stuff laying around. I felt awful and wanted to get out of there—one of those situations where you wish you had an ejector button to press so you can WHOOSH into the sky and go someplace else, fast. Where, I don't know. But I wanted to come, so I kind of took her by her waist and rolled her over onto her back. She was lit by the moon and she told me not to come inside her unless I had a Trojan which I didn't and she was crying and I came on her stomach and there were hickeys on her tits.

We got dressed without saying a word and then I told her I would drive her home in my father's car and she should really stop crying. We walked about five feet apart, stumble-bumming all the way. We were both tired. She said, "But I love you, I love you. I want to marry you. Why can't we get married? I want to have kids

with blue eyes and straight blond hair." Which is what I have. I
either didn't answer her or else just said things like, "Oh, Lorraine—"

We got to my house and got into my father's car. I had my own
keys and I hoped I could get her home and get back without my
parents noticing because I only had a learner's permit. On the way
to her house she said, "That was the best sex I ever had." I told her
she should call Tommy in the morning before she went to school
and tell him she had been drunk and was sorry and that nothing
happened between her and me. She didn't go for this idea, she
wanted to elope with me and move to California and I told her she
should go to bed and I would talk to her the next day.

When I got home my parents were both up and the living room
was full of cigarette smoke and my dog jumped all over me. His
name is Bob, not as in Robert but as in bobbing up and down in
water. My mother wanted to know where the hell I was with the
car, it was a school night and didn't I know what time it was, she
had to get up for work in the morning, and my father said that I
should have taken the registration with me and he went to bed. I
went into my room and locked the door and laid down on the bed
in the dark. The light coming in through the blinds made stripes
on the McCarthy for President poster and the male muscular chart
on the wall. In my mind the guy on the muscular chart became Al
DiCicco in a blue bulging nylon swimsuit with black pubic hairs
peeking out and curling back over the waistband. I felt up my cock
through my pants and it got hard. His jumped, stretching the
swimsuit. I pulled down my pants and briefs. My cock bopped out,
I swung myself onto the edge of the bed, gobbed on my hand, and
began. Al now stood in front of me. I reached out and felt the
weight of his balls through his suit. His adductors and abdominals
quivered, his cock sort of kicked, and the phone rang. I mean the
phone really did ring. As fast as I could I forced my boner back
into my pants which are quite tight to begin with and ran to answer the phone before anyone else did.

It was Tommy. My mother from their room wanted to know who the hell was calling there at two o'clock in the morning and I took the phone into my room and locked the door. Tommy was at Lorraine's house when I dropped her off, he said. Peeking out from behind the curtains, I guess.

"What the fuck were you doing with my fiancée all night long?" he wanted to know.

"We were just talking," I told him. "She was very upset and drunk and I was trying to convince her that you love her and she loves you." I rolled my eyes at this corn.

There was a pause. He was just breathing. Then he goes, "That's what she said." I could hear myself breathing also, into the mouthpiece and around and back into my ear. Paper was crinkling on the other end and then chewing with his mouth open in my ear and I could see the jaw muscles going and I said, "You have anything else to say, Tommy, or what?"

"I don't believe a word either of you lying fuckfaces say. I don't ever want to see your face again, Billy. I ever catch you within ten blocks of her I swear I'll blow your fucking brains out with my father's .45-caliber gun, I swear I will."

Then I said something like, "Go fuck yourself, shithead" or "Eat shit, you scumbag" or something or other and hung up. My mother was up again now and from the other side of the door wanted to know who the hell it was and I didn't answer her and my stomach started heaving but then I remembered Al, so off came the pants again and I finished the job with my left hand gripping his ass, my face buried in his pubic hair, and he shot into my mouth with a THWOOUP like when you spit real far. After a while I wiped the floor and my dresser with tissues. My mother has never once asked me what it is that causes the varnish to get eaten away like that in spots. I'm sure she knows what it's from, but holes would have to be forming in the floor and eating through to the ceiling of the basement before she'd say anything about it. If it was paint or ink or fingerprints she'd raise the roof but everything that has anything to do with sex is totally a taboo subject around that house.

Whenever I come home late, my mother—never my father—wants to know where the hell I was but I never tell her. I don't even know why she asks, because if I said I was with a girl I swear they'd both turn beet red and fall right over. I mean, I'll be watching TV with them, right? And a *bra* commercial will come on and you can feel both of them tensing up, practically holding their breath. Same thing if the word "pregnant" gets mentioned on some doctor show. And if two people are making out, *forget* about it. My father will pick up the newspaper or the *TV Guide* and start furiously turning pages, and my mother will suddenly say "Where are my cigarettes?" and get up and start tearing the couch apart.

I heard Bob scratching on the door from the other side and whimpering and I let him in and he gave me a slurp on the face and the next day my mother called up school sick for me and I took Bob to the park all day long, all the way over to City Island and Orchard Beach till we were both exhausted.

CHAPTER

2

I DIDN'T GO ANYWHERE NEAR RICE Stadium or the spot on the field where I was the night before with Lorraine. I could have gone to McCarthy headquarters to work but I didn't feel like it. I knew Al DiCicco would be in class.

There were a lot of people out with their dogs—mainly old-timers since it was a weekday. If you have a dog you can let him loose and carry his leash and throw a stick and things like that and I wondered what those old people would be doing with themselves if they didn't have their dogs to walk around with.

I walked along the top of the sort of toppled stone wall that borders on the bay shore at the foot of the sloping field. It was one of those spring days that couldn't make up its mind whether to be sunny or cloudy or cold or warm. Sometimes the sun would come out and I'd open my windbreaker and I'd think that I didn't really need it at all, and then the sun would go behind a cloud and a breeze would blow in off the water and I'd zip up my jacket and feel that I could stand a sweater on under it.

When I was a little kid my father used to tell me that the local farmers built the wall before the Battle of White Plains in order to keep the British out. In other words it would have been the Battle of Eastchester Bay or something if not for the wall preventing the British from landing, making them sail farther north. In one version of the story he had the British hightailing it up the bay to White Plains while the farmers, disguised as cows, scrambled up and down the shore taking potshots at the ships with blunderbusses and bazookas. Once I asked him how many British he shot and he explained that he himself wasn't around at the time. The basic story always sounded believable to me and for a long time I wanted to check it out, so one day a couple of years later I got the number of the Bronx Historical Society and dialed six digits and hung up and I haven't tried to verify it since then.

I continue to believe in my father's story of why the wall was built as firmly as I believe in the UFO we saw together one day when I was standing on the front stoop of the house, hanging on to the wrought-iron railing and gazing out at the water and up at the sky. My father was sweeping the sidewalk with a cigar in his mouth and in the sky there were only a few puffy clouds here and there. I saw a dull reddish-orange oval glob glowing and throbbing and silently gliding north to south. I hollered, "Hey Dad! Look!" and pointed. He looked up.

I was very excited and he was calm, just staring up at the thing in the sky, making circular motions in the air with the cigar in his mouth as if he was operating the UFO by remote control. I looked up and it was still there gliding along. No one else was around that I noticed. I stood on the milk box and again I yelled, "Hey Dad! You see that?" He just kept looking at it. I kept looking at it too and then it went behind one of the clouds and didn't come back out.

I ran down to him. "You see that thing? What was it?!" He picked me up and with the cigar still in his mouth he said, "I don't know. I never seen one that color." We both kept looking up at the cloud for the longest time but nothing ever came out of it. I asked him if he should call the cops or somebody and he said that there was no point to it.

I leaned against the rail on the Eastchester Bay bridge. Rifle shots echoed across the water above crisscrossing speedboats. The cops have a firing range on Rodman Neck which sticks into the water hiding most of City Island behind it. Down on the right are marinas and even a houseboat or two. Away in the distance the Throgs Neck Bridge crosses to Queens, hazy on the other side. You'd never know you were in New York City or the Bronx if it wasn't for the stolen stripped cars and beer cans and White Castle bags and stuff all over the place or the occasional used Trojan you'd step on.

I thought about Tommy and Lorraine and Joey and Roxanne and Sue and I figured I acted like a turd the way I sat in that cab and watched Sue run into her house crying and I wished that Joey had just driven us all home. I felt mad at him and sort of blamed him for everything that happened. I was pissed at Tommy and Lorraine for getting me into the middle of their fight and I felt kind of sorry for her if she really thought that was the best sex she ever had, which didn't say a hell of a lot for Tommy, that's for sure. It was exactly the third time I ever had sex with a girl. I was drunk each time, otherwise I wouldn't have done it, and I felt lousy each time it was over. I always figured the next time would have to be better. I'd go home and jerk off, imagining fucking around with Evan or Kevin or Evan *and* Kevin—the twins on my swim team—or several other guys, but Al DiCicco especially lately.

I passed the miniature golf course, the riding stable, went through the woods on the other side of the garbage dump beyond the firing range all the way to City Island and sat on a rock on this side of the bridge where I watched the boats and Puerto Ricans and black people fishing off the bridge. The sun was warm on my thighs through my dungarees and the rock was cold on my ass. I've never seen a single white person fishing off that City Island bridge except very old ones. A black man was yelling at his little kid, "Ain't no point to it. What you want it for?"

The fish the kid had just caught was too small in other words and the kid cried and screamed as if the man had wrung his pet dog's neck and thrown it in the water right before his very eyes. I didn't see anybody catch a single fish that day except this one kid. He got another nibble and he was all thrilled and excited while reeling in and then the father said it was too small and he threw it back and the kid got all upset and screamed and cried. I sat there for a good half hour watching this same scene over and over again and it never once occurred to this guy to let that kid keep one of those fish. I know my father would have let me keep one if we had been the type who liked to go fishing.

The rock through my dungarees got too cold and I walked through the woods to Orchard Beach where my father taught me to swim when I was a kid. We also used to go to the American Legion Club and my aunt's house on the Jersey Shore and Jones Beach and in the winter the pool at Columbus High School. When I finally learned to backfloat without sinking, he swung me onto his shoulders, I laughed and yanked his ears and he flipped me backwards into the water.

From a bench on the boardwalk I watched all the people and dogs go by. A truck was spreading piles of new sand around on the beach with a large kind of rake-type attachment. A barge was shoving up the bay and a speedboat was zipping and jumping around it, trying to be either real playful or a pain in the ass. Some dogs off their leashes came over to smell my feet or my knees or crotch and I figured that Joey had every right to stay at the Neck Inn for as long as he felt like. He didn't have to drive anybody home if he didn't want to and Tommy and Lorraine didn't purposely put me in the middle of anything, it just happened that way. I stopped feeling sorry for Lorraine because I didn't think Tommy was exactly holding his father's .45-caliber gun to her head forcing her to marry the one and only guy other than myself who she ever had sex with. I still felt bad about Sue, though.

A Great Dane jumped up on me and gave me a slurp on the face. I made up that business before about Bob the dog. I don't have a dog, and if you walk all over the park and the beach all day long by yourself you feel kind of dumb because you look like you're just wandering around with nothing to do.

I felt lousy. I guess I was hung over. Maybe I had delirium tremens which I heard about at a school assembly from a guest speaker from Alcoholics Anonymous. The thought of going to school the next day made me miserable because anyone who's absent on a Monday or a Friday has to stay after in the auditorium in order to be individually questioned and ridiculed in front of all the other absentees by the Dean of Discipline who is this sadistic turd named Father McNulty who everybody else seems to think is just the funniest cleverest guy on earth. There was no swim practice the next day either, so there was no reason at all to go to school. Swim practice is the one and only thing I like about that place.

*   *   *

It was drizzling by the time I got home. My mother was in the kitchen and my father was at the dining-room table reading the *Sunday News*. He's been a day behind as of last year. My mother said that supper was ready and the phone rang and she said whoever it is tell them you'll call them back or that she'd call them back if it was for her. It's never for my father. My mother has a lot of friends, though. She goes to the movies with "the girls" or to someone's house for coffee or to a card party at the Rosary Altar Society, but the only men my father knows are the husbands of my mother's friends who he only sees if there's a party or one of those corny adult dances with those lame bands like at weddings. And the only reason he goes is because my mother makes him. Well, she doesn't *make* him, I mean he could refuse to go if he really doesn't want to go but he's sort of become kind of a wimp in the last few years if you want to know the truth.

It was Joey on the phone wanting to know what happened to me that morning. He was going to the same school as me—Archbishop Hogan it's called—and we'd meet every morning and have breakfast in this coffee shop by school. I apologized for not calling to tell him I wouldn't be there. He asked if I was alright.

"Yeah, but I might not be there tomorrow either," I said.

"You sick?"

"Yeah. No. I'll tell you about it when I see you." I just didn't feel like talking to him, that's all. The second I hung up, my mother from the dining room said that Joey called before. The phone rang again and she hollered. My supper was getting cold. It was Al DiCicco asking me if I wanted to go canvassing for McCarthy with him that night. I said yes. He said he'd pick me up at seven. At a quarter-to I was ready. At five-to I started looking out the living-room window through the blinds. It was raining harder now so I didn't wait outside. I checked myself out in the full-length mirror behind my closet door which I had to buy out of my allowance because my parents thought it was ridiculous that I wanted one. I sat on my bed and bit a couple of nails. I heard the horn of his Kharmann Ghia and ran outside down the stoop into his car. He turned to me and said, "Hiya," put the stick shift into gear and kept smiling at me as we pulled out. I watched his hand on the shift, especially the muscle between the thumb and the index finger which is called the first dorsal interosseus.

CHAPTER

3

A FEW WEEKS BEFORE I MET AL, I was at a dance at Kathy's which stands for St. Kathleen's Academy for Girls. With Joey and Roxanne. I'm backtracking here a couple of months to April—the night I met this Sue who I mentioned.

Joey was saying, "Billy, what the fuck you lookin' at? Check out this piece, man."

She was checking me out quite thoroughly, probably thought I was shy or something the way I kept looking away from her, but what I was doing was looking at this guy about fifteen feet to her left wearing these very tight black pants—you know that stretchy kind with no pockets in the back?—facing the other way with one foot up on a folding chair, shifting his very fine ass, bopping it around to the beat of the music from the jukebox and that's why I kept looking away from this girl who Joey kept jabbing me in the side to get me to look at. "What a *fox*," he said.

We were sitting at a table in Kathy's cafeteria—Joey, Roxanne and me—feeling pretty good after having a couple bottles of Colt and a couple of joints in his father's car, the three of us in front, at our usual spot on this side street about a half mile away from Kathy's, which is in a no-man's-land, a former swamp near the Bruckner Interchange. Joey and I never went to Hogan dances. It's too far and I hear their dances are lame anyway. Priests walk around separating couples if they're dancing too close together.

We weren't crocked or anything, just nicely lit and laughing quite a bit at things like the amount of gum stuck under the table and various things like that which are a scream when you're in that state.

"She wants you," he said out the corner of his mouth.

I said, "Mm," as the guy switched legs on the chair. I looked at the girl, on a folding chair in a miniskirt with her legs crossed and long straight blond hair parted in the middle and down her back. She had what I knew was a very attractive female face and body. She was talking with a girlfriend and she kept looking at me and she was kind of feeling up her knee. The whole thing made me kind of nervous, I guess because I didn't have any desire whatsoever to talk to her or do anything at all with her. The only reason I was considering going over there was because although I had somehow gotten away with not having a girlfriend up till then, I figured it was about time I got one. Not that I wanted one, but everybody else had one—or was dying to have one. And this wasn't the first time Joey was doing this nudging matchmaking routine, either. He thought I was shy or lacked confidence or something. I like to dance and hang out and carry on with my friends, and those were the only reasons I had been going to dances at Kathy's—and a couple at Iona College with my fake proof.

So I got up and walked towards her, hoping that once I got a good look at her she'd have zits on her forehead or gnawed-up cuticles or hickeys on her neck or something like that but she didn't and she was looking at me quite eagerly as I approached but I didn't stop. I breezed right by her into the men's room and took a a leak, combed my hair, blew my nose, adjusted my crotch, tapped some Binaca on my tongue, came out and went over to her and sort of stood there with my weight on one hip and said hi.

She smiled and said hi and glanced at the empty chair next to her which her girlfriend had vacated while I was in the bathroom.

I sat down, my legs spread wide. "What's your name?" I said.

"Sue. What's yours?"

"Billy." I leaned forward with my forearms on top of my thighs and clasped my hands. This was to look casual. I glanced across to Joey and Roxanne. She was staring into space to the beat and he was intensely watching me with Sue.

I said, "You go to Kathy's?"

"Uh huh. You?"

"No."

"I didn't think so," she said. "I've never seen you around—around school. I've seen you at dances."

"I go to Hogan." Like I was proud of it.

"Ohh?" she said with a big pleased question mark. "I was at the last Hogan game—the last football game, against Thomas More." Hogan is a very jock school with a very jock football team and all that.

"I've never been to a football game," I said, "—to a Hogan game." I've never been to a football game *period* but if I said that she probably would have suddenly had to meet somebody or make a phone call or something. As it was, her face fell a bit and she said, "Oh."

I glanced around. The guy with the ass was gone. Sue wanted to know what year I was in.

"Sophomore," I told her and her face fell a bit more.

"So am I," she said and glanced away like she was about to start looking for someone else to check out.

I didn't know what I was doing there. I was thinking of a way to get away. I could go dance with Roxanne and sweat and everything, and I wouldn't be nervous anymore and I'd be back in a good mood. But I sat up, straight-backed in the chair, folded my arms, looked at her head-on and said, "I'm on the swim team."

She turned back to me.

"The varsity swim team," I said.

She smiled. She was back. I was relieved and disappointed.

"I didn't know sophomores could be on a varsity team."

"If you're good enough. I mean you have to try out and everything and usually if you're good enough they put you on the junior varsity but I made the varsity. It's quite rare."

She uncrossed her leg and it touched mine so she moved it away but then I brushed my leg up against hers and held it there. She didn't pull away, but I didn't feel anything. I mean I *felt* her *leg* but I didn't feel anything, if you know what I mean.

She wanted to know all about the team and what my sign was and where I lived and I asked her a lot of questions like that too, just to keep it even, so I'd seem interested in her and not conceited, although I know I must have sounded like I was bragging. I didn't like doing this jock imitation routine. Well, maybe I did, a little. I asked her if she wanted to dance and she said sure, so we went up to the gym which was the dance floor with a band playing and we danced a couple of fast dances which was fine but she kept looking around and waving to friends like she wanted to make sure they saw her with me.

There was a slow dance and she wrapped herself around me and she felt very hot and close and I went through the motions and did the things other guys do, like my eyes were closed and my head was touching hers but I couldn't get a hard-on no matter how I tried so I thought about Evan and Kevin, and then Paul Newman's kid brother in some movie I saw on TV popped into my head. Girls are always going wild over Paul Newman or Steve McQueen or James Bond or older people like that for some reason. I liked this brother of Paul Newman in this sort of western movie I saw that took place in the present. There I was dancing this slow dance with Sue, thinking about this guy in the movie and my head was on her neck and I could smell perfume but in my mind this guy is on a rumpled bed in his underwear in the ranch house that's in the movie and it's late morning. I, also in my underwear, sit on the bed and reach out, put my hand on his crotch and his cock jumps into my hand and he smiles out of one side of his mouth and I have a hard-on and I tried to grind up against Sue but there was nothing *down* there to grind up *against* and her tits were all mushed up against my chest. I lifted my head, looked up at the band playing on the stage and kind of choked, "I'm thirsty."

We went back down to the cafeteria where I butted in on a Tommy-Lorraine grapple, introduced them to Sue and got us two sodas. Lorraine and Sue already sort of knew each other. They were in a class together or something. Joey and Roxanne showed up and the four of us—me, Sue, Joey and Roxanne—left and we parked in this secluded spot he knew about off Shore Road right next to the water in New Rochelle by the golf course near the Pell Mansion. I think I may have mentioned that Joey's father's car is this big Impala so it has this huge trunk in which Sue and I had sex. I mean, with the trunk open. We had a blanket in there and everything and we were sort of half in and half out and I don't really remember how we managed it but we did, no problem.

CHAPTER 4

IT WAS A COUPLE OF WEEKS LATER, I guess, and I was walking by an empty storefront on Crosby Avenue after getting off the subway one day after school. There was a guy taping a sign to the inside of the glass that said:

24TH C.D
MCCARTHY FOR PRESIDENT
HDQTRS.
OPENING HERE MAY 15TH
VOLUNTEERS NEEDED!

I stopped on the sidewalk and watched him and he spotted me and froze and our eyes met and held for about three seconds. He had big brown eyes and brown curly hair and tanned hands with wide white fingernails and a big nose—not bulbous or anything—the kind when you look at it from the side, it curves out and down from the eyebrows without going in by the eyes, sort of like an Indian. Then he smiled with these very white perfect teeth. A flash. He didn't have much of a chin but when he smiled, a jawbone appeared like a V out of nowhere.

I watched him finish taping the sign and then I went inside. There was nothing in the store but a desk and five folding chairs, a phone and a map of the congressional district on the wall. He was unrolling a large black-and-white poster and I said, "You opening a McCarthy headquarters here?"

He nodded at the sign in the window and laughed, "Uh huh," and then he looked up at me with his big eyes, which sort of made me trip forward. He tapped the poster with his palm faceup and said, "They expect me to put this in the window." It was meant for inroading Kennedy territory—a smiling, shirt-sleeved Gene McCarthy shaking hands with a crowd of black people, an open johnny pump and a slum in the background. "The place would get bombed or torched or something." He looked at me. "You for McCarthy?"

"Yeah."

"How come?"

"Because I don't want to go to Vietnam."

"You want to volunteer?—to work for McCarthy, I mean."

"Well, I don't know, I have school and I have swim practice—"

"I was on my high-school swim team. What school you go to?"

"Hogan," I said to the poster.

"We're enemies," he laughed. "I went to the Mount." My school's archrival, Mount St. Matthew, which is in Yonkers. "Our season used to end in March," he said.

"So does ours but there's this big invitational in June. In fact, it's at the Mount."

"We'll whip your ass," he laughed again.

"I don't give a shit about that rivalry crap."

He nodded and looked down at the poster.

"I guess they think that's what the whole Bronx is like," I said.

"Well, they better wise up downtown if they think they're gonna win the C.D." He extended his hand. "My name is Al." I felt like I was about to be helped across a ravine or a precipice or something.

"Hi, I'm Bill." I took his hand and it was warm and firm and dry and so was mine and I was across. No one else knew me as Bill. Everybody called me Billy. "I don't know, maybe I could find some time now and then. I've never worked in a campaign before."

"Neither have I," he said, cracking a smile. "I'm getting three credits at school for this. I have to write a report about it." Then he quickly added, "Oh, I'm all for McCarthy. I mean, I would have volunteered anyway." He sat on the desk and folded his arms.

He was a sophomore at Fordham University, a pre-law major, and he said he was going to be the first Italian president of the United States.

I thought he was kidding. "Oh yeah? Can I be secretary of state?"

"Supreme Court's better. It's a lifetime appointment." He looked out the window. "Job security." This he said very seriously, like he was quoting someone. He slipped one loafer off. You could sort of see his toes through these stretchy black Ban-lon socks he had on. I started bouncing myself off a wall with my books behind my back. I could have left at that point but I didn't want to. "So, uh—" I said, "I guess you won't be back here till May fifteenth."

"Naw, I'll be here. I'm supposed to hang out whenever I have free time and enlist any volunteers who happen to stroll in."

"Sounds like a waste of time to me."

"Me too. I don't know who the hell they think is gonna volunteer from around here," he said, looking out the window again and raising his body in a quick bouncing movement on the word "here."

"So, I guess there wouldn't be anything for me to do between now and then."

"Well, you could—" He squinted at the ceiling and wrapped his hands around the edge of the desk. He started swinging himself around like on a gym horse. I got the feeling he was showing off. "You could help me clean the place up and enlist all the volunteers." He stopped swinging himself around and looked at me.

I quit bouncing against the wall. I couldn't think of anything else to do but go. Moving toward the door, looking at the floor, I said, "Okay, so—I'll see you around, then."

"Oh. Okay, so long. Will you be coming back?"

"Yeah," and I was gone.

That night and the next day at school I couldn't think about anything else but him swinging around on that desk with one shoe off.

McCarthy had done a lot better than anyone ever thought he would in the early primaries against L.B.J. Then after McCarthy tested the water and proved that it was okay to go in, Bobby Kennedy entered the race and L.B.J. threw in his towel. There was to be a primary in New York at the end of June between McCarthy, Kennedy and an uncommitted—alias Humphrey—slate, although Kennedy was not entered in our district. McCarthy came out against the War long before Kennedy, and McCarthy was against the Draft and Kennedy for it and the one and only reason I was having anything to do with any of this is because I want the War over by the time I turn eighteen. I'm scared shit if you want to know the truth. Practically everybody else in that school are all gung-ho hawks who think Vietnam is Iwo Jima or San Juan Hill or some other glorious military fantasy their fathers have told them about and they think we should drop atom bombs on Hanoi and Red China. The only reason I even went to that school is because my parents and most Catholic parents who can afford it think that only retards and junkies and niggers with switchblades go to public school. If you wear a peace button at Hogan some priest or brother tells you to take it off although it's okay to wear buttons for specific political candidates and mine is the one and only McCarthy button I ever saw in that place. I remember one RFK button on a black kid and a ton of Nixons. At Hogan they'd actually call you a faggot for wearing a McCarthy button.

After school I went by that storefront again and there was the sign in the window but the place was all dark and locked up with a gate. I was very disappointed. I wished I had asked him exactly when he'd be there next.

I used to jerk off all the time to guys, as I probably already mentioned. I mean, I still do. But I always used to wonder if I would ever actually have sex with anyone—a guy, I mean. When I first started jerking off, I knew I was supposed to be thinking about girls and cunts and stuff like that, which is what the other guys in the seventh grade were all going apeshit over. But whenever I did it, like in the bathtub mostly, and thought about girls, I wouldn't get a boner, or if I did get one, it was while I was thinking about those boys talking about jerking off—picturing them jerking off. They also used to talk about something called a 69 which I didn't know what that meant. Then one time when I was jerking off to me and Mario Omeara giving each other blow jobs at the same time, which is something I used to jerk off to quite a lot—two, three times a day at least—it finally dawned on me what 69 meant. But a 6 and a 9 are identical, only reversed, like two guys, not like a guy and a girl.

Anyway, I figured I'd be dead and buried before I got around to actually doing such a thing. I thought the only male human beings who thought like me were the ones in Greenwich Village that I had heard about who wore dresses and wished they were girls.

*　　*　　*

I went back to that office again the next day and the place was open and there he was sitting at the desk, poring over a huge pre-law book and papers. I went in. I said hi.

"Oh. hi." He sounded kind of excited. Then, like he was correcting himself, "It's so boring here."

He was working on a paper. I didn't know—I think because *he* didn't know—whether he wanted to talk to me or do his homework. "Maybe you're busy," I said.

"No, it's okay."

I sat down on the ledge by the window.

"At least it's quiet here," he said. "I can't concentrate at home." He told me he had two kid brothers. He tipped the chair back and by holding on to the desk with one hand he balanced himself back and forth on the two back legs of the chair. He asked me where I lived. In Pell Estates, I told him. He said he lived in Throgs Neck.

I had the *Village Voice* in my hand with my books. There was a cover story about McCarthy. "The *Voice* is really pushing McCarthy," I said.

"Yeah, I saw that. You really follow all this, I guess."

"Well, yeah, it's interesting."

"It's like a game," he said. "You know, with strategy and a finish and everything."

"But I really want McCarthy to win."

"Oh, me too."

Between then and May 15th McCarthy won the Wisconsin primary and the only volunteer other than myself was a retarded kid named Brendan. For two weeks Al, Brendan and I swept and mopped and cleaned that place up and rearranged the five folding chairs several times, which was Brendan's favorite job.

Al and I talked about politics. L.B.J. and the War. How Humphrey was racking up delegates in the non-primary states. The Republicans, Nixon and Rockefeller. We never talked about girls or anything like that. We touched on subjects like my school and what I thought about it, my swim team, his college. Sometimes we'd lapse into silence and it was never awkward, not for a couple of weeks anyway.

CHAPTER
5

THAT WEEKEND I HAD A DATE—MY first one ever—a double date with Sue and Tommy and Lorraine to the movies. But first I had to pick up Sue. I sat in an armchair for fifteen–twenty minutes which seemed like a week with the Yankee game on TV. There was Sue's father implanted in this recliner at full tilt, looking like he had been lowered into it by a derrick with glue on his ass or something. The *New York Post* was spread out all over him and there was one Chee-to on his chest and he was puffing on some gross cigar that kept making me cough, but does he put it out? No. He wanted to know what school I go to and what I want to be and what my parents do and things like that. Now you might say, Well, those are the kind of questions all parents ask boys who are taking their daughters out. But the thing is, he only asked them during commercials. Whenever one came on he'd say, "So—" while relighting his cigar, and he'd ask me some question with this tone 'like he was entitled to know the answer. I'd be in the middle of answering him and if the game came back on, he'd turn back to the TV and my sentence would sort of trail off or I'd finish it on Sue's mother who was in the other armchair all this while, hardly saying a word. She seemed pretty uncomfortable as if she too was a stranger in the house.

Then pop wants to know what my favorite baseball team is and I said "None," which of course was the wrong answer and he squints at me and chomps down on his stogie. Now I'll admit I could have said the same thing a little more tactfully like, "I don't really follow baseball," but I didn't exactly feel like being polite at this point. And anyway, I could have said something a lot more rude than "None" like, "My favorite baseball team? I'd have to go get a lobotomy before I could sit through a baseball game." But I didn't.

Sue's mom kept eyeing the newspapers and the Chee-to like she had asked him to pick himself up and make himself presentable before Susan's young man arrived. She kept stuffing and unstuffing a dish towel into the pocket of her housedress. Then she said to me, "Susan tells me you're on the swimming team at school, Billy."

"Yes, I am."

Dad grumbled something at the TV and she looked at him. Back to me she said, "That must be a lot of fun."

"Oh, yeah, it is, I like it very much." Then I went into my swim team spiel—sort of the same things I told Sue at the dance—how I'm only one of four sophomores on the team and how that's so rare and everything. Which never fails to impress the hell out of everybody. And it made her relax for a minute and she stopped being embarrassed.

My back was drenched and under my thighs from the plastic covers which were nailed onto the chair like upholstery, not just fitted over them like in Joey's house. The thought entered my mind that if my parents ever put plastic covers on their furniture I'd move out, I swear I would, or else never sit on them.

So I'm there trying to get unstuck from this chair which was impossible and I wished it had an ejector button on the arm so I could press it and go sailing out through a trapdoor in the ceiling like in James Bond movies, which as I think I may have already mentioned is a feeling I get quite often in a great wide variety of situations like this whole evening for example, practically every second of it.

Something particularly spectacular occurred on the Yankee

game and Sue's father went wild from the torso up. He looked like a paraplegic or something the way his butt and legs didn't budge in that recliner but Sue told me he works in holes or ditches or something for Con Ed. So while he's going ape over the game Sue's mom asks me if I would like a Coke and I said that yes I would please. So she brings me this very nice Coke in a very tall glass with lots of ice and a piece of lemon in it and it was fizzing out the top so you could tell she just opened the bottle. I had never heard of putting a piece of lemon in a Coke before, believe it or not, and I liked the way it tasted and told her so and her face sort of lifted like a saggy curtain rising to reveal a beautiful view, and this was the best part of the whole evening. I drink quite a lot of the stuff and ever since then I've been putting a piece of lemon in it, and whenever I do I think of Sue's mother who was quite a nice person.

Sue finally made her entrance and we left.

Maybe you think I'm rude or a smartass the way I'm talking about Sue's father, and maybe you think I was disrespectful to him while I was there. Well, see, I don't believe in any of that Respect-Your-Elders crap. He was rude and disrespectful to *me* from the second I stepped foot in that house. And if you ask me, telling someone to respect your elders is the same exact thing as telling a black person to respect a white person, for instance. People's age doesn't have anything to do with it and most kids take too much shit from adults just because they're adults.

THE DAY OF THE ARRIVAL OF THE
McCarthy people I skipped school and had my friend Emo forge
an absence note. She possesses the very sellable ability to forge
people's handwriting perfectly, with hardly any practice, and she
has my mother's down to a T.

As I was walking down Crosby Avenue towards the office a bat-
tered bus with a huge dirty blue-and-white McCarthy for President
sign on it passed me. I ran and beat it to the office. Al, Brendan
and I stood outside like a welcoming committee and watched the
people get off. They had been through primaries in New Hamp-
shire, Wisconsin, Ohio and some other places like that. Half of
them looked like people in this program on Channel 13 about
Appalachia that I once had to watch for school and the other half
looked like WASP versions of Al DiCicco. They wore cordovan
penny loafers and Al wore black Italian slip-ons with tassels. Their
shirts were Oxford cotton button-downs and Al's were European-
cut with darts in the back that made them skin-tight which looked
very good on him. He had a swimmer's body like mine.

Al introduced himself and us to the guy who seemed to be in
charge and he responded with a grunt and, "Maybe you can help
us unload."

We took maps, charts, chairs, computer printouts, file cabinets,
boxes of campaign literature, buttons, bumper stickers, posters and
McCarthy shopping bags—some filled with a ton of other stuff—
out of that bus. In twenty minutes you could hardly move in the
store.

This guy in charge had nicotine stains on his fingers, crud under his fingernails, a ponytail down to his ass and black horn-rimmed glasses. He pronounced "garbage" as if it rhymed with "cabbage" and his word for "shopping bag" was "sack." We found out that his name was Harold only after someone addressed him. He got the keys from Al and asked him where the file of volunteers was.

"What file?" Al asked.

"The file of volunteers," he repeated a little louder.

"Bill and Brendan and I are the only volunteers."

Harold looked at Brendan and then at me and he rolled his eyes, which I didn't exactly appreciate. He turned to look at the map and then Brendan imitated him rolling his eyes and Al and I thought that was pretty funny. Harold removed his glasses and wiped them with a piece of E-Z Wider.

Al said, "The downtown office told me to just sit here and enlist anyone who happened to stroll in. They said this was a low-priority district."

"Terrific." Harold put his glasses back on and scrutinized the map.

Al went on. "It's a very conservative area. It's the only part of the city that has a Republican state senator and assemblyman."

Harold was still squinting at the map. "Other than Richmond County," he said, which was the first time I ever heard anyone refer to Staten Island as Richmond County. "I know all about the district," Harold said. "I've studied the demographics." He lit a cigarette, shook out the match and, scanning the busy roomful of workers, continued to flick his wrist as if the match hadn't or wouldn't go out. He turned to Al and me and said, "Here, why don't you take these sacks and distribute this literature at Farrell High."

"Where?" Al asked.

"Farrell High School." He tapped the map with an index finger and left a smudge mark.

I looked at Al and said, "Kathy's." Monsignor Farrell High School has been called Kathy's for as long as I can remember. It used to be St. Kathleen's Academy for Girls. It went coed about two years ago and I guess they figured they couldn't send boys to a school named for a female saint so they changed the name in honor of some dead principal or somebody, but no one seemed to care or notice and no one has stopped calling it Kathy's.

Al and I looked at the flyer, which was aimed at recruiting student volunteers. Among other things, it referred to McCarthy's anti-War, anti-Draft, pro-aid to education positions. Al and I looked at each other and he said to Harold, "What do you think this is, Cambridge or something?" He knew and I knew that dropping those flyers down a sewer would produce as many volunteers as handing them out in front of Kathy's.

"We've recruited hundreds of thousands of students with that piece," Harold said.

"Maybe in Boston or Madison but not in the Bronx," Al said. "You don't know what it's like here, you just got off that bus."

Harold stuck his chest out a bit. "I'm the Senator's representative in the district," which made me think of the relationship priests supposedly have with God. "Our priority right now is to recruit volunteers for the Candidate."

"You're not going to recruit any volunteers that way," Al said.

Harold wasn't pleased with us. "Well, you can help these people set this place up, then—if you'd like," which is what Brendan and everybody else were doing.

"You want to go to Kathy's?" Al asked me.

I couldn't tell what he wanted to do. I took a stab at, "Okay."

"Let's go," he said.

I wasn't exactly delighted with this idea because I knew people in that school—like Lorraine and Sue—and they'd never understand me having anything to do with this McCarthy business. We got into Al's red Kharmann Ghia and drove over to Kathy's. He took the main entrance and I went around to the side. It was a quarter to three. At three the bell went off and kids flew out of that building screaming like it was on fire, which is something you wouldn't do at my school. You have to act "with utmost decorum" within a five-block radius of Hogan, which is one of about a million rules there which if you ask me are all unconstitutional but they get away with it.

I felt like a jerk handing out those flyers. Hardly anybody took one and those who did either laughed or threw them on the ground or both or called me a faggot or things like that. Distributing campaign literature for a left-wing candidate, you were begging to be called a faggot.

After about fifteen minutes I went around front where Al was furiously handing out flyers, getting the same basic reception I had gotten. I went over to him and said, "This is a waste of time."

"I know."

"Let's go."

He stopped and looked at me and said, "Why don't we hand them all out." I figured he wanted to prove a point to Harold, so I went back around to the side and I thought I saw Lorraine and I cringed but it wasn't her. When the tidal wave dwindled to a trickle I went back front. Al was picking up flyers that everybody had thrown all over the place and I helped him.

It turned out that no one was right and no one was wrong because in the next week we got about eight volunteers from Kathy's and then Harold sent us back there again.

After we brought the extra flyers back to the office Al asked me if I wanted to go for pizza and I said sure. We went to the Gold Star restaurant which is dimly lit with wooden-backed booths behind your head, so it's not your basic pizza-shop hangout. You might bring someone there on a date after a movie. It was Al's idea to go there.

By dimly lit, I mean everywhere except right over your table, which is the one spot you might really want to be dimly lit, they've got these low-hanging lamps that are green on the outside and white inside that are too bright and low so as you sit down you almost bump your head on them.

Al and I had never been together anywhere except hanging around that office preparing the way for the May 15th arrival. We talked about Harold and the other jerks in the office—how they got right off that bus and set that place up without skipping a beat, without stopping for a single minute to stretch their legs or take a piss or have a cigarette or just stand around or nothing. Then out of the blue Al asks me how many brothers and sisters I have.

"None," I said.

He was kind of hunched forward with his elbows on the table, his shoulders tense.

"How about you?" I asked.

"I have an older sister and two younger brothers."

"Oh, right. You told me."

"I didn't tell you I had a sister."

I couldn't think of anything to say to that.

He was sort of picking at this blue-and-white checkered tablecloth.

I looked up at the wall at a painting of Venice that must have been done by a relative or friend of the owner, all done in lovely puke shades of yellow, green and brown, and I said that I bet you couldn't find colors like that in Venice if you tried. My hands were in my lap. Actually I was holding on to the insides of my thighs for some reason, like in a dentist's chair.

Now he was flicking Italian bread crumbs against the wall. The waiter showed up with our sodas and Al abruptly sat up straight, put his hands on his hips and with great interest watched each glass being placed on the table as though they contained some kind of exotic brew that he never saw before.

I asked him where in Throgs Neck he lived.

Again he started digging at the tablecloth. "On Schurz Avenue. It's a two-family house. My grandmother and grandfather live downstairs."

He didn't look at me very much but I didn't take my eyes off him. When he did look at me our eyes would hold for a few seconds longer than you usually hold eye contact with someone. Not just longer—like probing, like when two people have the same thing on their mind but neither one wants to be the first to spit it out. And then, as if the words that wouldn't come out our mouths were about to surface on our eyeballs, we'd look away in different directions, him at the oil and vinegar and me at the jukebox, for example. Or at the other people in the place or the chef in the kitchen who you could only see through a window from the neck down and the stomach up. Or the waiter who was this guy who had been working there forever, on the phone by the bar talking Italian with his back to us, gesturing wildly with a cigarette. I thought he was arguing but then he laughed real loud and long, flicking ashes near an ashtray on the bar. When our pizza came up he put the cigarette and receiver down, brought the pizza over and said, "So everything okay, boys?" We said yes and he went back to the phone.

Al said, "So you're an only child, huh?"

"Yep."

"What does your father do?"

I didn't like talking about this stuff at all. "He's a—" I know I turned red, "—an A & P manager."

"What's wrong with that?"

"Nothing. My mother is a legal secretary. For a lawyer."

"Oh, yeah? My father's a construction worker. A bricklayer." For a second he looked at me like, You gonna make something of it?

Chewing, I lied, "That sounds interesting."

He laughed. "Where in Pell Estates do you live?"

"Why."

"You live in one of those mansions?"

"What mansions."

"Down by the water."

"You call them *mansions?*"

"Well, what would you call them?"

"I don't know—big houses."

"You live in one of those big houses?"

I put a half-eaten slice onto the tray. "I wanna get out of here."

"What's the matter?"

"I just wanna go."

"*Why?*" He was leaning forward, instantly changing his expression from slit-eyed smug to wide-eyed apologetic, pinching the pizza tray.

"I don't know," I said.

"I was just—" He started to pick apart a piece of crust. "Everybody from Pell Estates acts like it's Scarsdale or something."

"Well, they don't really believe that. Anyway, I don't."

He unscrewed the glary light bulb.

"My parents bought this house before I was born," I said, "when there were still a lot of vacant lots. It's a very small house. On Ohm Avenue. At the corner of Watt."

"Oh, right by the park."

"Uh huh."

He didn't crack the usual stale joke about "What street?" He asked me if I had a dog.

"No, my mother says she doesn't want dog hairs all over the house."

"There are dogs that don't shed."

"Yeah, I know. She says she doesn't want the dog shitting and pissing on the carpet."

He was pushing ice cubes to the bottom of the glass with the straw, trying to keep them from rising to the top.

"You know—when it's a puppy," I said. "Being trained and everything."

He wrapped his fingers around the glass and looked at me with his big eyes as if he was trying to read my mind or something and he says, "Sometimes my whole family goes away for the weekend to my sister's house in Jersey City." He seemed to be getting closer to what he was trying to say or trying to find out. "I don't usually go with them." He kept flexing his first dorsal interosseus. "And I have the whole house to myself."

I sort of tried to change the conversation. "I have an aunt who lives in New Jersey. In Sea Bright."

"Oh, on the Shore."

"Yeah. Right on the beach. With three dogs. She's on the town council there and everything."

"What is she, your mother's sister?" He loosened his grip on the glass and relaxed his shoulders.

"My father's dead brother's wife. He got killed in the Korean War—my uncle did." I stopped feeling like I had to read something between the lines of everything he was saying. "She says she can get me a summer job there as a lifeguard."

"Oh yeah? I have to get a summer job too."

"Well, I don't really *have* to. But I might. I like it down there."

"My father wants me to be a hotshot politician," Al said. "He's got connections with certain people who could make it easy. And I could get a good summer job too, but I don't want anything to do with them. My father's really from the old school. A real *paisan.*"

"So you mean you don't really want to be president?"

"Oh no, I do. That was my idea. But not the way he wants."

Without saying so, we agreed to shelve the unspoken topic for now and, relieved that the strain had lifted, we blabbed on.

In front of my house in the car he turned to me and smiled and said, "See ya."

I opened the door and hesitated for a second. I looked at his knee and then at him and I said, "So long." Once I was inside, the car slowly pulled away.

Pell Estates is a perfectly nice neighborhood and everything, one- and two-family houses of all different shapes and sizes, some very old and some *are* actually mansions that were built when it was part of Westchester County which is a fact the old-timers around there are very proud of. But a lot of people who have moved there recently are into doing things like covering the front of a red brick house with fake flagstone or putting Blessed Virgin Marys in their front yard with a spotlight on them or paving the front yard with concrete or various things like that.

My mother wanted to know why I didn't call to say I'd be late for supper. I said I was sorry, I forgot, I already ate. She said I could have the consideration to call so she wouldn't make supper for me and waste food.

I took a bath and imagined making out with Al in his Kharmann Ghia, feeling up each other's crotches. It was a very long bath because next we were suctioned together in a sleeping bag in the woods with a campfire and crickets and everything when my mother knocked on the door to say Tommy was on the phone. I said to tell him I'd get back to him. That guy's got radar or something, I swear. I think I called him back the next night.

CHAPTER
7

AT A QUARTER TO THREE THE NEXT day at school the dismissal bell rang and, as usual, you'd think the teacher had just found a cigar box ticking in a desk drawer or something the way everybody bailed out of that room and bolted in various directions toward lockers or exits—without actually running because if you run and get caught by an S.C. they report you to McNulty and you get detention the next day. These S.C. shits would actually report you too, it wasn't just some idle threat that hangs over your head. The student council is this very honorable association of stooges, McNulty's rats, which you attain if your marks are good enough and if you *want* to be on it. One time I saw this kid running down a hall and three S.C.'s gunned after him and knocked another kid into the wall in the process, and if the purpose of the No Running rule is so that—well, you get the idea.

My last class was nowhere near my locker, which was real annoying on the days I didn't have swim practice because I needed to get out of that place as fast as possible. It's like when you stay underwater to see how long you can hold your breath and when you feel like you'll burst you surge upward and you know that in a couple of seconds you'll be able to breathe but you can't breathe yet and then you explode into air and you inhale through your nose and exhale through your mouth and your body feels good and your chest and you swim and swim in a very mighty easy manner. Going out the exit door of Hogan was like that sort of, only without the exhilarating part. Sometimes I'd actually realize after leaving the building that I had been holding my breath. But that day I had practice so there was plenty of time to kill and it wasn't frustrating not to be able to tear through the halls.

My locker alcove on the fifth floor was jammed—a tight noisy mob scene. You were allowed to make up for the rules against running, pushing and shoving by yelling and howling as loud as you could. I hung out against the opposite wall and waited.

Hogan is on very rocky hilly ground near the Harlem River, so when you enter the building through the front entrance you're actually on the third floor. The classrooms on the second and first floors have windows in the back and on one side that look out to the river which is filthy but the bridges are arched and graceful and there are cliffs on the Manhattan side. Below the first floor is B level where the gym is and the pool is on C. From the fifth floor it took at least fifteen minutes to get down to the pool and that's if you were moving at a fast clip.

When there was enough room I took what I needed from my locker and headed toward the pool. On the unused stairwell that I always took, the yelling and pounding subsided, became muffled, then stopped as I walked through a maze of drippy corridors on B, went through a door marked BOILER ROOM—NO ADMITTANCE and took the shortcut down a dank catwalk to C. More leaky corridors lit by weak bare bulbs. I caught the first faint scent of chlorine as I turned a corner and was back in a brightly lit main corridor. At the end of it was the entrance to the pool.

Through the swinging doors that say PO on one and OL on the other, from the balcony above the bleachers that look out and down to the pool below, I saw Evan and Kevin stretching out on a mat on the floor. I walked straight toward the locker area and my head kept turning to hold the view. They were doing leg stretches in phase and as they stretched toward and bounced over their toes, their hair, red brown and very straight, flopped up and down, flashing red gold from light shafts penetrating huge high windows. Mr. Bieniwicz always saw to it that those windows were kept clean.

They caught sight of me looking at them as I went past and they smiled with white overbites. I waved and smiled and they waved. It's always kind of humid in there.

They had freckles and gray green eyes and slight overbites that weren't buck teeth or anything and I was glad no one ever bothered to get braces for them. Kevin had a slightly chipped tooth in front which he got when someone's head collided with his mouth in freshman year during a dodgeball game at gym. They always took gym even though you don't have to if you're on a varsity team. I never did.

I turned into the locker area. Nobody ever calls it the locker room, it's always the locker *area*. I think it has something to do with this very plushy gray carpeting they have in there. I wasn't exactly dying to see Mr. Bieniwicz because I knew he'd be pissed about my missing practice the day before, the day the McCarthy bus showed up.

I passed various guys getting changed and I said hi or waved or nodded and they said hi or waved or nodded or said yo. One thing I never say is yo. I've tried it a couple of times but I don't like the way it sounds on me.

All the way at the end I turned right. That's where the coaches and gym instructors have their office, this big gray beat-up room that looks like it was transplanted from a navy destroyer. Papers and dead footballs and bats and bulletin boards crammed with notices from the year one and trophies and things are always all over the place. There are about ten huge gray metal desks in there that look like they weigh about a ton each and seated at one of them in the far left corner wearing only his blue-and-gold swimsuit, a blue tanktop and his whistle was Mr. Bieniwicz staring out the window. The shade next to his desk was the only one in that office that was ever open. He was leaning on the desk holding his head, scrunching up his brows and clicking a ballpoint pen, his whistle occasionally swinging lightly back and forth like the pendulum of an irregular clock. He's about twenty-five, a Hogan alumnus. I once looked up his picture in an old yearbook in the school library. He looks better now.

Everyone calls him the Bean or Beanie or Beanball or Beaniebags or about fifty very clever and brilliant variations on that idea. Including me, I have to admit, whenever I was with a group of guys who were talking about him. I'm going to call him Mr. Bieniwicz here, though. In order to call him the Bean and be real natural and cozy about it you'd also have to be into constantly talking about smacking your ham and hitting the ceiling or fucking pussy or eating it or how far you can piss. You'd have to be forever walloping other guys' bare asses with wet towels in the drying room and laughing and carrying on about it in a corny, supposedly unsexy way. Evan and Kevin never called him the Bean, not even around other guys. Those two didn't care what anyone thought of them.

Mr. Bieniwicz's hair was wet and combed straight back with a few strands hanging over his hand. The leg that was visible was bowed under the chair, his foot bent at the toes with his heel in the air. On the other side of the room were two gym instructors— older, middle-aged, hammy overweight bulldozer types standing with their legs about ten yards apart, laughing about some hysterically funny story, swinging their hairy meat hooks at each other. They're one of the main reasons I never took gym. They're the kind who'll say, "Okay, fifty squat thrusts," and then demonstrate *one*. *Maybe*. They couldn't do two if they tried.

Mr. Bieniwicz turned and saw me standing in the doorway. "Oh," he said. "Come in, Connors." He moved a couple of papers around.

"Sit down," he said.

There was one of those little stand-up calendars on the desk with X's through the used-up dates.

One of the gym instructors let out with a window-rattling guffaw. Mr. Bieniwicz stood and signaled for me to follow him. We kind of moseyed through the locker area. His arms were folded and without looking at me he said quietly, "What the hell happened to you yesterday?"

"I was sick. I'm sorry."

"What was the matter?"

I changed my story and told him the truth about the whole McCarthy business although I didn't mention a thing about Al. He seemed to understand and we talked about it like we were just there to shoot the breeze.

"I worked for Bobby Kennedy," he said, "when he ran for senator in '64."

"Oh, really? Who'd he run against?"

"Keating, the incumbent. It was a close race and—you know, ordinarily the in-man has the edge, but—"

"He probably got a lot of votes because his brother just got killed the year before."

"Yeah, true, but Johnson's coattails helped pull him through. I wouldn't admit that then."

"You don't get involved with politics anymore?"

"No—I don't have the time." Then he changed his tune and said, "Listen, Connors, you have to take your responsibility to the team a little more seriously. I can see how the campaign is important to you but you know the invitational is in just a few weeks. You've made a commitment to the team and it's not right to spread yourself thin like this."

"But I want to do both."

"Well, there are only twenty-four hours in the day and if you've got your fingers in too many pies you have to make a choice, even if both the things you're involved with are worthwhile, honorable things. You wind up having conflicting loyalties, and both will suffer. You should have a sense of loyalty with your teammates. Fealty—"

Fealty. Twenty-four hours in the day. Fingers in too many pies. Right. Through most of this I kept my eyes on his whistle and every now and then I'd look up at him and he would refocus and miss a beat, as if he became ever so slightly self-conscious about what he was saying. He started fingering his whistle and said, a little louder and a little deeper, "Alright, go get changed right away and do some extra warm-ups. I want to see you sweating when I get down there."

That killed me. I mean, it was no big deal, I knew he wasn't actually going to verify whether I was sweating or not, but it was the kind of thing one of those slob bulldog gym instructors would say. You could tell he felt slightly ridiculous saying all that stuff too, as if it was somebody else's idea of something that *ought* to be said for my own *good*.

He went back in the office and I turned into the alcove where my locker was and there, about ten feet away, was a bare ass bent over like I was getting mooned. I said, "Hi, Sandy."

This was Stanley Sandrowski, picking his toes in the buff. He didn't look up. If you lined that whole team up and had them moon me, I swear I'd have no problem identifying one and all. He put his foot up on the bench so that his balls swung in the breeze.

He kept picking at his toes. "The Bean was all bent outta shape yesterday y'know, that you missed practice."

"Yeah, yeah, I saw him already." I opened my locker and on the top shelf was a roach walking around on my honey bear. Swimmers eat things like honey and M & M's and gelatin before a meet, so I've got this plastic honey bear that I squeeze into my mouth and here was this roach taking this very casual stroll all over it. It didn't even run away or anything or freeze when the light hit it or nothing.

"What are you doing digging at your toes?" I said.

"I'm not *dig*gin' at my toes, I got a fuckin' ingrown toenail'r some shit."

"Bad?"

"Yeah, it's bad. It hurts. Waddaya think?"

"Did you go to a foot doctor or something?"

"Naah." He slipped his suit on and sat on the bench, adjusting his balls. He picked his foot up in his hands and stuck his toe out and bent over it so he could scrutinize it more closely. It was all red and sore and pretty gross. "The Bean tol' me to see a doctor but when the fuck am I supposa have time between yesterday'n today?"

From the looks of it, it seemed to me he must have known about it for at least a week but I didn't say anything about that. I took my towel out of my gym bag and hung it on a hook. They provide towels for you but they're like diapers and the soap smells like lard or something so I always kept my own in my locker, as well as toothpaste, toothbrush, comb, deodorant, Desenex, baby powder, Bufferin and Band-Aids. There's something about the whole procedure of using all that stuff that I like. Several other guys also had a lot of that junk but some, Sandy for example, never had a single thing and then they'd ask to borrow your comb or something and when they were done with it they'd very non-chalantly hand it over encrusted with dandruff and crud and say "Thanks" real casual-like. Although that's mainly the kind of thing that happens in regular gym. There are very few slobs on that team, I have to admit, but I don't lend my comb to anybody anymore and I don't care what they think or say about it.

"Why don't you go to the school doctor?" I said to Sandy.

"Waddayou, re*tard*ed? You couldn't *drag* me to that fuckin' quack. If I was *dy*in' in the *street* in a pool of my own fuckin' *blood* I wouldn't—"

"Well, maybe you should stop *dig*ging at it."

"I'm not *dig*gin' at it, fuckin' Connors, I'm tryna *drain* the fuckin' *pus* out of it, awright?" He wasn't mad at me, he was mad that he had the ingrown toenail.

Then he did something that really impressed me. He pulled his foot up to his mouth and started sucking on his big red pussed-up toe. Now don't get me wrong. If you have an ingrown toenail I'm not saying you should gobble away at it and down the pus but ordinarily I wouldn't think there was anything wrong with putting a toe in your mouth. I really wouldn't. Most people think things like that are gross and disgusting though, and I don't think Sandy could have known that I wasn't one of them and here he was slurping away on his big toe right in front of me, not giving two shits what I thought about it. I have to give him a lot of credit. He stood up with a sound of disgust and slammed his locker shut and left. I told him I'd see him down at the pool. He didn't say anything.

I had my suit on and put my goggles and noseplugs around my neck. The roach was now doing a balancing act on the very tip— the opening—of my honey bear. I tossed the whole thing in the garbage and went down to the floor and started to do some stretching exercises. There was Sandy, swinging all over the place on a rope. Evan was spotting Kevin doing sit-ups and then while I was doing body crunches they switched and saw me. I was looking at them upside down and I said hi. I've never seen two such happy guys in my life. Talk about fealty. They were always happy and I don't mean in a dumb mindless way like a lot of people are supposedly happy. I mean these two always looked contented and really delighted about whatever they were doing. They seemed as interested in geometry as they did in ancient history, for example, and usually you're miserable in one or the other—like geometry. I didn't think either of them would be able to stand it if anything ever happened to the other one. They were crazy about each other. I don't mean in an erotic way. Well, maybe I do. I don't know. But if their relationship wasn't sensuous I don't know what you would call it. At practice they'd always smile at each other and be real playful and slap each other's asses in wet swimsuits, which by the way has got to be one of the best sounds on earth—that wet smack. Very often I'd be dying to slap their asses and slip my hand in there and feel them up. Swimmers, including me, usually have pretty good-looking asses but Evan and Kevin's were exceptional. I mean, you could set a case of Coke on their glutes, no problem. And the elastic that curves around the bottom of the cheek—you know the way it usually rides up and exposes a couple of inches? On most people the elastic sort of squishes the skin in a little bit, right? Not on them. Not the slightest impression.

Sandy started yelling like Tarzan and swung himself off the rope, almost landing on top of me, somersaulting all over the place. Evan, Kevin, Sandy and I did this tumbling routine we had been working on for months. Very acrobatic. It didn't seem to bother Sandy's toe. Most of the team was there by now, so we were showing off. Mr. Bieniwicz showed up and we did the Circle and then warm-ups—more cal than usual—and in the pool he had us do a thousand free instead of eight hundred but I didn't mind. Swimming is the one time I can ever sort of turn my brain off and think of nothing and feel very vital and vivid in full exertion and it's painful and strenuous and if you're healthy you sail and glide through and go and go and go out and out and it's much better than real life.

Mr. Bieniwicz whistled time out and we sat on the sides of the pool with our legs in the water and talked about the invitational and he warned us about the Mount's slippery walls. Our pool is cement and theirs is tile in other words. We were breathing and he was walking around with his arms folded talking about what we did wrong and who was looking and who was loafing it and he said, "Sandy, did you go to the doctor like I asked you?"

"Uh, no . . ."

"Why not?"

"Well, I—um . . ."

"Your timing was way off. Let me look at it." Sandy boosted himself up and Mr. Bieniwicz went over to him, squatted down and looked at his toe. "Go shower and change and wait in the balcony for me, okay?"

When we finished the workout we did the Circle again, which is something I doubt any other swim team does. You sit around in a circle like Indians and clasp hands and close your eyes and chant these sounds that are supposed to make you harmonious or something. I'm not putting it down. I liked the way I felt when we did it. It was very—I don't know—idyllic. And to tell you the truth, I really liked the holding hands part, depending on who was on each side of me. But I'm not sure about the harmonious business. I got the impression from Mr. Bieniwicz that he wished there was less competition within the team. Not competition. I mean everyone was real cooperative at practice and even more so at a meet, but as soon as practice or the meet was over the seniors stuck together, the juniors stuck together, and there were only four of us sophomores and no freshmen. It's unusual for there to be any sophomores on the team at all, never mind four, as I think I might have mentioned already.

Hogan doesn't have shower stalls, just one large room with shower heads. Some seniors were going berserk in there to the extent of pissing on each other and soaping up and wrestling all over the floor or things like that which are actually quite sexy to watch sometimes but if I ever partook I know I would have wound up with a hard-on in the middle of the shower room. I usually got in and out of there fast.

A couple of them in the locker area were bad-mouthing the Circle and calling Mr. Bieniwicz a faggot and maybe that's why it was never completely harmonious. Any time I ever hear anybody getting called a faggot it's for the wrong reason. I never got called a faggot unless it's for wearing a McCarthy button or not lending somebody a comb or various other very brilliant reasons like that. There were several priests in that place who would swish around in their cassocks like they wished they were nuns and you never heard anybody calling any of *them* faggots. But Mr. Bieniwicz would get called one for doing the Circle.

Someone told me he's a conscientious objector, all official and everything, and that's why he's not in the army or Vietnam. When he was running that fealty line past me and I looked him in the eye and he refocused, I think he might have sensed that I could see he didn't really believe in it but wished he did. Or that he used to believe in it and wished he still could. Or that he still did but had yet to come across it.

I looked for Sandy but he was gone. I went over to Evan and Kevin who were both knotting their ties and I asked them if they knew what Mr. Bieniwicz said to him. They always knew everything.

"He sent him to the school doctor," said Evan.

"But he didn't want to go," said Kevin.

"Did he go?" I asked.

"Uh huh," they both said.

I was forever hearing rumors about them being incestuous and things like that from guys who didn't even know them. They got called pretty insulting things right to their face but they didn't give a shit. I don't mean they just pretended not to give a shit, I mean they truly did not care what anyone thought about them. They were completely—well, perfect. Together.

MY FATHER WAS WATCHING TV IN
the living room when I got home and my supper was heating on
the stove on a plate on a pot of boiling water with an aluminum
bowl over the plate. I went past their room where my mother was
putting on makeup at her blond vanity table. I said hi. She said hi
honey. I went into my room to get undressed.

They had been arguing. I knew, I can always tell. It hangs in
the air like an exploded cherry bomb and on their faces and fake
relaxed poses. They argue a lot—not much when I'm around, but
very often I'll show up and you can tell they've been arguing very
fiercely right up to that second.

"Your aunt called," she hollered from their room. "Call her
back tonight. It's about the job. And Tommy."

"Okay."

Then, with a forced pleasant voice she said, "How was practice?"

"Fine," I said to the smoke that was wafting out of their room. I
hate it whenever they ask me how was practice because they never
come to any of my meets. My father used to, when I was a freshman on the junior varsity. But once I made the varsity he stopped
coming. I never asked him why.

There are a lot of mysterious things that I suspect about my
parents—things that never get spoken about when I'm around—
invisible topics that sort of cling to the walls around that house but
no one ever brings them up. Not when I'm around, anyway. Like

I think they wanted more children and couldn't for some reason have any. Or one of them wanted more children—I don't know which one—and the other one didn't. Also, my mother is ten years younger than my father—they got married when she was eighteen years old and she had me nine months to the day later. What I'm saying is that I think she's tired of being married to him. Maybe he's getting old too fast. I don't have any proof for any of this but I believe it pretty strongly anyway.

I called my aunt. She said I should come on down there that coming Saturday to take this written test and lifesaving classes and some other stupid things like that— this all-day thing that would start at eight in the morning. I said sure and that I would take the bus down Friday night if that was okay and she said she would meet me and everything.

As I entered the kitchen I said hi to my father. He said hi. I placed an open book on the dining-room table and sat down and ate.

My mother came in and said that she was going to Evelyn's for coffee. She took her keys and cigs off the counter. "There's cranberry sauce in a bowl in the fridge. Didn't you see my note?"

"No," I said to the open book which may have been upside down for all I know because it was geometry. I always keep a book open in front of me so it looks like I'm preoccupied. Supper was this turkey roll stuff that comes frozen in the shape of and solid as a log and it doesn't look like anything that was ever part of a turkey. A tree maybe. With Heinz Great American Gravy on it.

My mother stood there for a second and I knew she was looking at me. She lit a cigarette, put it in an ashtray and went to the refrigerator. "How many times do I have to ask you not to walk around this house in your underwear?"

I can *never* walk around that house in my underwear. Lucky for me I don't have any hair on my chest yet, but if I ever do I'll have to shave it or wear a shirt all the time buttoned to the neck. Maybe

I'm exaggerating a *little* but I really think she finds the fact that I'm growing up, that I'm becoming a man, that I'm a sexual being, an embarrassing thing. She wishes I was still a kid. They both do.

She got the cranberry sauce and put it on the table. "Go put on a robe or your pajamas."

"I'm going out." I was cracking the knuckles in the toes of my left foot.

"Where."

"Canvassing." I wasn't going anywhere, I planned to do homework.

"Never mind canvassing. You spend too much time with that. I don't know when you have time to do your homework."

Even though I knew she had heard my whole end of the phone call, I said, "I have to go down to Aunt Margie's Saturday—Friday night—about the job."

"Oh? Okay." Which is what I knew she would say, pretending she hadn't been listening.

I didn't touch the cranberry sauce. I kept eating what was on the plate, looking at the geometry book like I was real engrossed in it, cracking the knuckles in my toes.

She said, "I'll be back around ten," went to the front door and said to my father, "I'll be back around ten." I didn't hear him say anything but then she said, "Evelyn's," and was gone.

I dumped the cranberry sauce on the plate and finished eating. I washed the dishes and called Tommy and he asked me if I wanted to go to the movies Friday with me and Sue and him and Lorraine.

"You mean tomorrow?" I asked.

"*Next* Friday."

"That's over a week from now."

"People make plans, you know."

This dating thing was pretty new to me. "Yeah, well, to see what?"

"*I* don't know," like it was a very dumb question. The other time we double-dated, Tommy and Lorraine didn't really care what we saw. We sat in the balcony and the two of them practically fucked right there, so it doesn't really matter to them what's showing.

"Well, it depends on the picture," I said. "I wouldn't mind seeing *Planet of the Apes.*"

"That sounds okay."

I didn't get around to asking Sue about it till the following week.

I spent quite a lot of time that night writing Al DiCicco's name in the back of my ancient history notebook a million times with all different colored Flair pens and in all different various artistic ways.

I kept wanting to call him but I didn't have anything specific to say. Finally it dawned on me that we had planned to go canvassing Saturday.

I had him in my address book in pencil under his first name with "McCarthy" next to it and in pen under his last name which was added a couple of weeks later.

"Hello." It was his father.

"Hello, is Al there?"

He held the receiver down and hollered, "Al!"

I heard Al somewhere in the distance: "*Now* what?!"

"*Don't NOW WHAT ME, mister smart aleck, I'll smack your face! TELephone!*"

Al's father was the official phone answerer in that house. This was the fourth or fifth time I called there and he answered every time. The first time when I asked for Al, he said, "Junior or senior," and I took a stab at junior. I guess he recognizes my voice now.

"Hello?" It was Al.

"Hello, Al?"

"Yeah—oh, hi!"

"Hi!"

"Waddaya doin'?" he asked.

"Oh—nothing—homework."

"Me too—trying to."

A pause. He didn't say What's up or anything like that. There was a TV on in the background and then a dog barking and a couple of kids laughing and screaming. I said, "Did you go to the office today at all?"

"Nah, you?"

"No. Listen, Al, I have to go down to Jersey Saturday."

A woman was yelling in the background. "Papa! Don't bring the dog up here wichyou. I ask you a thousand times—" Then she started to say something in Italian.

"Billy, hold on a second," Al said. He carried the phone into his room. I don't know what he'd do in that place if he didn't have his own room. I tried to picture what he had on. If he had no shirt on or bare feet or just underwear or what. This is something I did every time I called him.

Then he whispered, "I thought we said we'd go canvassing Saturday—you know, you and me."

"Yeah, I know, I want to, I mean I'd rather do that, but I have to go down there and take some tests and stuff for that lifeguard thing—you know the job I told you about?"

" . . . Right."

"I just found out now. My aunt called—"

"Good. So, uh, how ya doin'?"

"Fine, I'm just doin'—homework."

"Oh yeah? What?"

"Geometry."

"Ugh." We laughed, then I heard his father and his brothers again in the background but I couldn't tell what they were yelling about. Al said, "So, I guess I better get off."

"Oh, okay."

"Thanks for calling."

"Um—"

"Bill?"

"Yeah?"

"We can go canvassing Sunday," he said.

"*Yeah.*"

"Okay?"

"Definitely."

"So, ah, I'll see ya then, okay?"

"Ten o'clock?" I asked.

"Yeah."

"Okay. Bye."

"Bye." A soft click.

I took my hard-on into my room and I actually jumped up and down and then did fifty push-ups and fifty jumping jacks. Sue and them were the furthest thing from my mind. I took a shower and laid down in the tub and soaped up my cock and beat off to "Me and Al in 69 in the Woods by the Fire."

CHAPTER 9

WHEN I WAS A KID I WOULD GO down to my aunt's house with my parents once in a while for the day, like on a Sunday. But lately, the past couple of years, I've been going there by myself for a weekend, mainly during the summer. She likes to have me down there. I just go swimming a lot and lay around in the sun and get a tan and sometimes ride bikes with her or have a barbecue or things like that. And she never treats me like a kid. I mean she treats me like a *kid*, but not like an inferior dope which is what most adults think the word kid is the same thing as. And she never says things like Do you have a girlfriend or Do you like girls or What's your girlfriend's name or

You must break all the girls' hearts, like various other relatives used to say to me all the time. My aunt has never once said anything like that. She's asked me about school and the team and I know I've told her about Father McNulty and Mr. Bieniwicz and Tommy and Lorraine and Joey and Roxanne.

That Friday night when she picked me up from the bus—she's got this white Jeep Renegade—we went home and we were eating this whole smoked chicken she got in the mail from the Ozarks or someplace and we were talking while we were eating and she asked how was the swimming going. I remember telling her about Evan and Kevin and describing exactly what they looked like and she said, "They sound really cute," and I said, "Oh, they *are*," and she looked at me and I froze with food in my mouth and she smiled and winked.

CHAPTER

10

HAROLD'S IDEA WAS FOR EVERY-body to work their own neighborhood because if you were able to say "Hi I'm Joe Schmo and I live around the corner" people would perk up their ears and listen to you. I'm not saying it wasn't a good idea. It made sense but I didn't want anyone I knew seeing me doing this. I mean, it's considered a very faggoty thing to ring doorbells with campaign literature and say, "Good evening, I'm working for McCarthy for President." If any of my friends ever saw me, they wouldn't know what to make of it. I had already said all this to Al, and so we always did areas on the other side of the C.D. Westchester Square, places like that. He understood, although according to him he didn't care who saw him doing what or where.

On Sunday he picked me up at five to ten. I told him about the lifeguard tests. Everything had gone fine. I was best in everything and I was definitely hired and I was to start on the last Friday in June.

There were several people standing around in the office. Which is just about all a lot of those volunteers ever did. It was a social club for a lot of them, an excuse to get out of the house.

Some of the so-called liberals in that office were forever talking about civil rights for blacks and grape pickers and everybody and in the very next breath they'd crack some faggot joke. If McCarthy ever heard them he'd tell them to go fuck themself, I think.

A few days later Harold had us go back to Kathy's with more recruitment flyers. I took the same side entrance again because I figured if Lorraine and Sue didn't come out that way the last time, they wouldn't this time either.

I was handing out those flyers and all of a sudden there's Lorraine and some girlfriend of hers—not Sue—on the steps. There must have been at least three other exits so of course they decided to come out of that one. I wasn't going to hide behind a bush or anything, so I just kept handing out those dumb-ass flyers and then Lorraine spotted me and the two of them came over and Lorraine said, "Hi, Billy. What are *you* doing here?" One eye was looking at me and the other one appeared to be real interested in whatever was going on over my shoulder.

I gave them a flyer and I kept handing them out and they looked at it as if it was written in Chinese or something. Then they looked at each other like people in comic books with question marks over their heads and the other girl said, "Who's McCarthy?" and I said, "He's running for president." Then Lorraine goes, "You mean of the United States?" I couldn't immediately think of a brilliant answer to this so I just said, "Yeah."

"How come *you're* doing this?" Lorraine wanted to know. "You getting paid?"

"Yeah." It was easier that way. They both seemed kind of re-lieved by this explanation.

"Where's Sue?" I asked, forgetting that they weren't really friends to hang around together.

"I don't know. You called her about Friday night, right?"

"No." It was Tuesday.

"Well, you better call her. She's very popular around here, you know," she said kind of with a huff.

"I'll call her tonight."

"Anyway, me and Tommy had a fight so I don't even know if we're going."

"You'll go."

They were about to leave and I sort of eased Lorraine over to the side and said, "Lorraine, look, don't mention this to Tommy or anybody—that you saw me handing this stuff out."

She looked at me and said, "You're not really getting paid, right?"

"No."

"What are you doing it for, then?"

"Because I want to."

"You want to?"

"Yeah."

"Why?"

"Because McCarthy is against the Vietnam War and I don't want to get drafted, okay?"

"Well you don't have to get all snotty about it."

"I'm not gettin'—oh, you don't understand, Lorraine." And she left.

I imagined saying, "Because I have a crush on this guy who works in the McCarthy office, Lorraine," which was the second reason. Or maybe it was the first.

After Kathy's, Al and I went canvassing door to door together. Harold preferred male/female pairs because according to him, peo-ple were more inclined to open their doors to a man and a woman, but there were more men than women working out of that office anyway.

This was a couple of days after Kennedy beat McCarthy in the Nebraska primary. We talked about the campaign and agreed that McCarthy had to win in Oregon the following week or he could pack it in.

Later, in his car after leaving the office to go home, I asked Al if he felt like going to the Gold Star. He sort of punched me on my thigh and said sure.

I told him about the upcoming invitational and we talked about swimming in general. His best stroke is the fly and mine is breast. I was telling him what warm-ups my team does before practice and then we got on the subject of the Universal gym and he said that his favorite muscles are the thighs. "The rectus femoris and the vastus lateralis."

"I like where the obliques meet the iliacus," I said.

"Oh yeah, that's great."

"The way it slopes down to the abdominals."

"Right."

We were really getting excited talking about this and the area around our table seemed to be getting heated up and then as I was sipping on my Coke through a straw he said, "Do you like to look at yourself in mirrors? You know, full-length mirrors?"

I think I must have blushed or choked on the Coke or both because it so happens that I do like to look at myself in full-length mirrors as I might have already mentioned, especially when I'm wearing my team swimsuit, which is a blue Lycra Speedo with a two-inch wide gold vertical stripe on each hip. Without taking my lips off the straw I looked up at him. "Yeah," I said. "Every now and then." I sometimes get a hard-on watching certain guys at practice—Evan and Kevin for instance—and if you want to know the truth, I actually get a hard-on every now and then from looking at *myself* in that swimsuit. Which is what was happening right there in the Gold Star.

Al was pulling at a long gooey piece of cheese with his teeth. "So do I. Sometimes. Like when I have a swimsuit on."

That pizza must have been unusually sloppy that night because we made some mess of that table. We stopped talking. We sat there with our eyes kind of glued together. Without actually coming right out and saying certain things, we understood each other. It wasn't just understanding, though. It was like we were floating on our backs in a bay or some place like that and occasionally a wave would roll us leisurely up and down, in unison. In other words, if the wave had feelings it would have thought we were part of the same person. Or that we were part of the wave. Or that we were the wave.

CHAPTER

11

THE NIGHT OF MY SECOND AND next-to-the-last date with Sue rolled along. Another double date with Tommy and Lorraine to the movies.

My father was going to do the weekly food shopping at the A & P where he's the manager, so I asked him to drop me off at Sue's. I didn't tell him whose house it was or where I was going and he didn't ask. You know in the movies when a kid tells his father that he's going on his first date and the father acts all proud with his chest out as if someone had just told *him*, the father, that he was the most manly he-man alive? And the father slaps his kid's back and says "My son, you are now a man" and tells him about Trojans and stuff and maybe even gives him a few? Well, not only would my father not do any of the above stuff, he would—if I had said, "Dad, I have a date tonight with this girl Sue,"—well, I don't know *what* he would have done. I mean I just wouldn't have *said* anything like that to him. Not that I wanted him to be all thrilled over the fact that I was going out with a girl—I didn't even *want* to be going out with a girl. It's not that. I wanted to be able to talk to him about how I felt about *guys*—the same way we used to talk about the Battle of White Plains and UFOs. But there's a wall between us that started getting built around the same time I started beating off and by now it's about ten feet high and six feet thick. And even if there *wasn't* any wall I could never have told him how I felt about guys. I mean I don't know a single guy who talks to their father about anything other than sports maybe, or who's going to take the garbage out or mow the lawn or when *he* was a kid or other very weighty things like that. And my father passes out if there's a *bra* commercial on TV, remember?

Anyway, in the car I thought that I would rather have been a kid again going with him to the A & P and ride on the front of the wagon. He'd push me around and let it go flying and I'd laugh like crazy and he'd run and grab it if he thought I was going to crash. Everybody used to say hello to him and to me and one of the cashiers always gave me candy bars from broken bags. He was the assistant manager at that time.

The scene at Sue's was basically the same as last time. On the bus to Fordham we sat Tommy Lorraine Sue Me and I was watching these two little kids sitting across from us, real comfortable together on one seat, with their mothers on either side of them chatting over their heads, holding on to their peewee coats.

The boys had chocolate all over their mouths and hands and shirts, their feet only reached to the edge of the seat and there was a piece of bubble gum stuck to the bottom of one of their sneakers. They were gawking all around like they had never been on a bus before. The one with the bubble gum had a teddy bear who had chocolate all over *his* mouth and the other guy had a G.I. Joe wearing only his helmet and one boot, and he looked like the Viet Cong had tried drowning him in a vat of melted Hershey bars or something.

I was trying to catch their eye but I couldn't, then finally I did, by rolling my eyes, going cross-eyed and making a million faces and sounds with my cheeks and tongue and weird things with my fingers which are double-jointed. They were gaping at me with great interest now, and then one of them starts smiling and dribbling and hitting his teddy bear and laughing and the other one starts laughing and sort of pushing one foot with his other foot and he drops his G.I. Joe on the floor and decides to start mountain climbing all over mom, grabbing her blouse and her tits while I kept making all these faces and noises. She pushed his hand away from her tits and then the two moms finally caught on to what was going on and they smiled at me and down at the boys and then resumed their chat.

In a couple of minutes they all got up to get off the bus with the women carrying the kids who were craning their necks gaping at me, making dribbling noises like they didn't want to go and smacking their moms in the eye, trying to climb out of their arms and everything. So I waved and winked but they didn't wave, they just kept straining and gaping at me with all their might with their heads bouncing. Then I spotted G.I. Joe on the floor. I jumped up, grabbed him, hollered "Wait a minute!" and they stopped and turned and I tried to give the G.I. Joe to the kid but he didn't even want it, he just scrunched up his face and turned red and started wailing as loud as he could and mom smiles and says, "Oh thank you," and takes it and the other kid was staring at his pal like he wanted to know what the hell he was crying about and they got off the bus. I kept looking after them through the window and those two kids' heads were still craning after that bus and bouncing all over the place swinging the teddy bear and G.I. Joe all around with all their might and this business with these two kids was the best thing that happened that night.

I sat back down next to Sue and she was smiling at me and so were several other people, but not Tommy and Lorraine. They hadn't noticed any of it, I don't think. Sue took my hand and held it all the way down Pelham Parkway up Fordham Road to the

RKO Fordham. It was a problem trying to think of anything to say that we hadn't already talked about. She told me about things like this garden club she belongs to at school where they plant trees and flowers and rock gardens and things and vegetables all around Kathy's which was kind of interesting even the second time around, and she sings in this glee club that goes around to old folks homes and places like that, so I hope I haven't given you the impression that she was a complete airhead or something. She wasn't. It's just the situation, the circumstances of the way we were together, this dating thing, that I didn't like. Like if I was on a bus with Joey or Emo or even Lorraine alone, let's say, you could ride without uttering a single word except maybe cracking a joke every now and then or making some witty comment about someone on the bus, and if there are long pauses of silence it wouldn't make a bit of difference in the world.

Fordham Road is a pretty hideous place. Definitely the filthiest and most garbage and it's always windy around there, blowing newspapers and crud down this long hill. Beer cans roll around and hit your feet. When I go to the movies with Joey we always go to New Rochelle because he gets his father's car.

We sat in the balcony—Tommy Lorraine Sue Me—and the place was filled with mostly kids our age yelling and making out real passionately and feeling each other up and everything all over the place and popcorn was flying and the air was as sticky as the floor.

I could tell that Tommy was pretty absorbed by this picture *Planet of the Apes* because he kept whispering real loud things like "Quit it!" or "Because I'm trying to watch the fucking picture, *that's* why!" and various things like that to Lorraine which of course caused a huge argument and people started telling them to shut up and they stormed out to the lobby, holding hands while arguing.

There was a girl in front of me with her boyfriend's arm nice and comfortable around her. He had on a white tanktop and had very nice shoulders and arms and beat-up hands with dirty finger-nails, the kind like a construction worker can't get clean, and even in the dark I could see these very rough fingers making small gentle massaging motions on his girl's back and it sort of made a wave pass up through my chest and around the sides of my neck and made my ears hot and I wanted to feel his deltoids. I put my arm around Sue and there was hair all over her shoulders so I had to move it and eventually my arm fell asleep so I removed it. She shifted around in her seat sort of displeased while I massaged the pins and needles. I asked her if she wanted anything to eat and she said she could go for some Bon Bons. I went to the lobby and there's Tommy playing pinball, with Lorraine nowhere in sight. I went over to him and he said that she was in the ladies room crying or having a period, I can't remember which. I bought the Bon Bons and went back in and gave them to Sue. I decided to forget about kissing or putting my arm around her and just watch the picture which was quite good.

There was this scene where this guy gets captured by the apes and put in a zoo and he's just got on these rags with a tan sweaty body with nice muscle tone and they whip him and beat him and stuff and this gave me a hard-on. Don't get me wrong. I'm not condoning those apes whipping and beating this guy. But if you want to know the truth, with him sweating and squirming all around this cage in his flimsy rags was quite sexy.

Tommy and Lorraine managed to catch the tail end of the movie and then we were outside the theater trying to figure out where to go and eat, and he suggested we go back to Pelham Bay to the Gold Star but I said I didn't feel like going there, so we went and had Chinese food on Fordham Road. We splurged and took a cab home. Tommy said his parents were away for the weekend so the four of us went to his house and Tommy and Lorraine went into his room and I had sex with Sue on the couch in the living room.

Which brings me back to where I started this whole thing—the party at Tommy's in June and fucking Lorraine on the field by the water and not going to school the next day and walking around the park and Orchard Beach and leaving in Al's car to go canvassing with him in the rain. That all happened the following week.

CHAPTER

12

BECAUSE IT WAS RAINING, AL AND I decided to canvass an apartment building. Actually we didn't even finish a whole one although we probably spoke to more people than when we did regular houses. Afterwards we went to the Gold Star which by that time was a regular thing, at least for a soda. We were both in a good mood. I said, "Al?"

He put his arms on the table. "Yeah?"

"I wanted to ask you, uh—would you like to come to our invitational on Saturday?"

He grinned. "Sure."

We talked about the invitational and about the strong new possibility of McCarthy winning the California primary, which was the next day. It had looked grim, but our man's standing in the California polls rose sharply after he trounced Kennedy in Oregon the previous week, and if he won California it would give him momentum coming into the New York primary which was in two weeks.

Then, out of the blue, he says, "You have a girlfriend, Bill?" He tried to make this sound real casual, but it was something we had never talked about. In situations like that you have to decide in a fraction of a second what to say and it seems that at least half the time you say something that later on you could kick yourself for. I looked up at him and said, "Yeah. Why?"

"Oh, I don't know. No reason."

It became awkward like the first time we were there. Why, I don't know. I told the truth. I was going out with Sue. Each time I went on a date with her and brought her home which I dreaded because I knew she'd expect me to make out with her and feel up her tits and things like that which I absolutely had no desire to do, so I'd give her a peck on the lips and say goodnight and she'd stand there looking at me with this odd look on her face as if she thought that she personally was the problem. Which is what happened the night we saw *Planet of the Apes*. That story about Tommy's parents being away for the weekend and Sue and me having sex on the couch in Tommy's house was complete bullshit in other words, as perhaps you guessed because that parents-away-for-the-weekend business I don't think was one of my more imaginative creations, and I only thought of it because of Al DiCicco's parents who really do go away for the weekend occasionally to Jersey.

We really did take a cab home from Fordham Road, though.

Tommy and Lorraine got out a few blocks from Lorraine's and then Sue and I got out at Sue's. The yellow stoop light was on and the only light inside was from somewhere in the distance like the kitchen or someplace, and there was nothing going on in there that I could hear. Sue opened the door, reached in, shut out the stoop light, sat down on the steps and looked up at me and her mouth kind of twitched. I think she was smiling. I sat down next to her. Her tits were moving up and down and she was waiting.

I said, "That was a pretty good picture, don't you think?"

"Uh huh."

"Some makeup job they did."

"Yeah, it was."

"The way the mouths moved and everything." Then I sort of imitated one of those apes but Sue didn't think it was so funny. She moved closer to me. I lifted my arm. I put it behind her and touched and held on to her shoulder while I kept my eyes glued to a crack in one of the cement steps. My hand was wet and it was ejector button time. I turned my head and faced her and her lips parted and her eyes sort of half closed and I kissed her on the lips and I didn't feel anything. I didn't like the taste. Or her smell. Or anything. I removed my arm, stood up and said, "Well, I have to go, I guess."

Her eyes widened and the sides of her face fell a few feet. She must have thought she was ugly or that her tits weren't big enough or something like that and I wanted to tell her it had nothing to do with her, that I didn't want to feel up ANY tits and I didn't want to make out with ANY girl and I thought cunts were GROSS and she shouldn't take it personally and I left feeling like a total jerk and angry at myself for not at least going through the motions of making out and feeling her up and things like that. After all, how awful could it be? So I walked all the way home and on the way I wanted to crawl into the nearest sewer and drown and die, and I got home and laid on my bed in the dark and stared at the venetian blind shadows on the guy on the muscular chart whose hands are sort of outstretched the way Jesus Christ's hands are in some pictures. I wondered if I was nuts or a pervent or that maybe I should have been a girl and that thought made me even madder because I like being a guy, I like my body, I like the way I feel about Al and various other really attractive sexy guys like Evan and Kevin. I have to tell you I feel perfect physically if you want to know the truth. And so my brain my mind what I think and feel why should that be any different. When Evan smacks Kevin's ass in a wet swimsuit is GREAT, I like I love the way it is about me and Al and I got a hard-on and jerked off and fell asleep with my clothes on and my fly open and tissues on the floor. So when Al asked me if I had a girlfriend and I said yeah, it was really a lie and I think that's when I realized about *their* truth and *my* truth and it became awkward, probably because he was trusting me to tell him my truth and he knew I was lying. He said, "What's her name?"

I told him and then I said, "Do you have a girlfriend?" I was hoping that he wouldn't lie too. He looked me in the eyes and my head moved a little closer to his, sort of the way I tripped forward towards him the day we met. He said, "No."

The words "Neither do I—I lied" repeated inside my head and inside my mouth over and over again but they wouldn't come out, and they just kept repeating and I think my lips were actually moving slightly as if the words were trying to pry my mouth open but I fought back and looked away and the words "I'm tired" came easily out of my mouth. Then we left.

When we got to my house he said, "See ya," but he wasn't smiling and he seemed kind of drained or something. I opened the door and hesitated. I opened it wider and turned and looked at him. He looked at me and our eyes and heads moved towards each other and I shut the door of the car. Our mouths slightly opened and our eyes gradually closed and I think he actually sort of smacked his lips—or maybe I did—and then BULL'S-EYE!

I opened my eyes so I wouldn't miss a thing and his eyes were closed an inch away from mine and one of the best things was the smell. And the taste. And I swear I could have died right then and there. We heard a car and his eyes opened and we pulled away from each other and the headlights flashed by. His right hand took my left hand and our two hands sort of felt each other up very slowly, feeling the muscles in our hands, our fingers, and we just sat there watching them for a while. The skin on the whole palm side, including his fingers, was smooth and taut and the pads on the palm right below the fingers were hard.

He started to talk and his voice was kind of husky and he cleared his throat and said, "My family's going to Jersey this weekend. After the meet you could, uh, come over if you want to."

I WENT INSIDE SORT OF TRIPPING over myself realizing what it was like to really KISS. My father was watching the Yankee game in the living room. He doesn't have a recliner though, and he's not a slob and he doesn't like Chee-tos. He likes to eat fruit. Mainly apples and pears. He loves pears. Especially when they're kind of overripe and bruised. My mother was on their bed doing her checkbook, which means that all kinds of papers were all over the bed with a haze of cigarette smoke suspended over it and she said that Lorraine called, which gave me a thumb-pressed-on-the-chest feeling.

I stuck my head in the room. "What did she say?"

"To call her back."

"How did she sound?"

She looked up and exhaled smoke as she said, "What do you mean, how did she sound?"

"I mean, how did she—forget it." I took the phone into my room and stared at it for a while. I undressed. I smelled my hands. The left one smelled different—and better. I tried bending my head so I could smell my neck, which is something like trying to look at your eyes in the mirror without looking yourself in the eye, although unlike with the eye business, I was able to get a good whiff.

I dialed six digits of Lorraine's number and hung up. This was the very next night after Tommy's party and the business in the park with Lorraine, remember. I dialed the whole number, it started ringing and then she answered it. "Hello?"

"Hi. Lorraine?"

"Billy?"

"Yeah. How ya doin'?"

"Awright." Pause. "How are you?"

"You called here before?"

"Yeah."

"How's Tommy? Did you talk to him?"

"He's fine . . . Sue wanted me to call you."

"Sue wanted you to call me?"

"Uh huh."

"What do you mean she wanted you to call me?"

"Just what I said."

"What for?"

"I don't know."

"What do you mean you don't *know*?"

"Well, I *know* why she wanted me to call you but I don't know why she couldn't call you herself. I said to her—"

"That's what I mean—"

"She was real bitchy and sarcastic to me on the phone and everything."

"What did she—?"

"I said to her she should call you herself."

"So what's it about?"

"She's breaking off with you."

I was delighted and annoyed. "She told you to call me to tell me that?"

"I told her she should call you herself, I mean I don't like being in the middle of it, you know."

"She tells you to call me to tell me she's breaking *off* with me?"

"Billy—"

"What *balls*. You'd think we were going *steady* or something. We went on *three fucking dates*." I was glad that the farce game with Sue was over.

Lorraine went on. "She says you won't kiss her and you don't find her attractive and since you find *me* so attractive—this is what *she* said—she doesn't see any point in—"

"Fine. You can tell her that's just fine. You can tell her that she just beat me to it, that's all—"

"We're not speaking, how am I supp—"

"—By about two hours because I was going to call her tonight myself and break off with *her*—"

"You *were?*"

"Yeah, so as far as I'm concerned it's a mutual thing, so you can just tell her that."

"I don't want to argue with you, Billy."

"Yeah—okay."

We both just breathed.

I said, "So how are you and Tommy?"

"You said last night that you would call me today."

"I *did* call you. I just called you, didn't I?"

"I called you first."

"I just got home. I was going to call you whether you called me or not." I can't remember if this was true or not.

"You *were?*"

"I'm standing here dripping. I called you the second I got in the door. As I was dialing the phone my mother told me you called."

"Really?"

"So did you talk to Tommy or what?"

"Yeah."

"And what."

"And what, what?"

"What's the story with you and Tommy."

"I don't want to talk about it."

She was really annoying me. Al popped into my head. Forget about these dooshbags. "Okay, fine," I said. "Do you have anything else to say?"

"Um, well, I don't know."

"Okay, so long then."

"Bye, Billy."

I had the receiver halfway between my ear and the cradle and I heard a scratchy "Billy!" come out of the earpiece. I pulled it back to my ear. "Yeah?"

"Never mind. Bye." And she hung up.

I wanted to call Al. He probably wouldn't be home yet so I took a shower and while I was in there it dawned on me that I was washing his smell off me and that made me feel lousy. Then I called him.

"Al?"

"*Hi*. Uh, wait a minute." I guess his father was out, although there was a lot of noise and talking: women's voices. I could hear him carrying the phone someplace else. A door closed. "Hi," he said. "How do you feel?"

"I feel fine. I mean—great. How do you feel?"

"Great. Great. I've been thinking about you—ever since I left."

"Yeah?" My eyes, my face I knew were very bright. "I've been thinking about you."

"Yeah?"

"Uh huh."

"That's really nice."

"Yeah." Then I said, "Al?"

"Yeah?"

"Uh—"

"What?"

"I just wanted to tell you—"

"Can you hang on a second?"

"Yeah." Then I heard him say "—Yeah well *I'm* using it. *Wait* a minute." Then, "That's *tough*. *Wait*." Then back to me, whispery, "Yeah. Hi."

"Hi."

"What were you saying?"

"I wanted to tell you that I don't have a girlfriend. I lied before in the Gold Star."

*   *   *

Lorraine is the only girl I've ever had sex with and it was just that one time—on the field that slopes down to the water—if that even counts as sex which it doesn't and if you want to know the truth I don't plan to have sex with girls anymore. And you know that business about fucking in Joey's father's trunk on Shore Road next to the water by the Pell Mansion the night I met Sue? I made all of that up too. Sue and I were in the cafeteria with Tommy and Lorraine just like I said, and I looked around for Joey or Roxanne but couldn't spot them anywhere. Lorraine and Sue were chewing the fat and Tommy and I were shooting the breeze and for some reason I recalled when I was a little kid being pushed in a stroller at the Bronx Zoo by my father who was shooting the breeze with a man next to him pushing a stroller with a kid in it who I was blabbing with and we were throwing elephant food at each other and up ahead of us were our mothers walking and chewing the fat.

Finally Roxanne showed up, and then Joey. I was relieved. They don't really act like a couple, they act like two separate people. I didn't introduce them to Sue. Joey said they were leaving and I told Sue that he was going to drive me home. She looked at me and frowned and everyone else got quiet. To smooth it over, I asked her for her phone number and she gave it to me and she said she had to find her girlfriend and she left. Joey and I went to take a leak.

At the urinal I said, "Why don't we go to the Neck Inn? The three of us?"

"I don't know," he said. "I don't really feel like it. Me and Roxanne are probly gonna go to Orchard Beach parking lot or someplace." He was zipping up his fly. "Shore Road maybe."

I was trying to check myself out in the mirror from behind some guy puking into the sink.

Joey said, "You know, you and that chick could've come with us, you know, but you didn't look like you wanted to, so I didn't say nothin' about it."

"I don't feel like it."

"Well, we're gonna go park at—"

"Yeah, okay. You'll drive me home though, right?"

"Yeah."

"Okay, let's go," and I left the bathroom.

I had one leg up on the backseat of the car and Roxanne was in front sitting sideways with her left arm on the back of the seat, kind of looking back and forth at both of us.

They dropped me off and I went inside and my ears rang in the silence. In the kitchen sink in an ashtray a broken lipstick-smeared cigarette was trying not to go out. Their door was closed and not a sound came from behind it. I went into my room and undressed. My shirt smelled like Sue's perfume. I stuffed it in the hamper in the bathroom and washed my neck and chest and shoulders with a facecloth while I stared into the mirror and the mirror stared back and my reflection kept becoming someone else and then me again. I don't mean it *looked* like anybody else, it was me exactly, nothing changed visually, just in my head my reflection at times is not me.

I sat on the toilet in my briefs, stared at the radiator and saw the guy with the ass at the dance. I leaned back, closed my eyes, spread my legs, flexed my thigh muscles and watched them flexing for a while. I stood up, turned on the dim light over the sink and shut off the overhead, sat back down and—well, you get the picture by now. The following week I met Al.

Maybe I'll rewrite all this and unscramble everything and take out all the lies and put everything in order so it makes sense. I'm not going to lie anymore.

CHAPTER

14

June 4, 1968

Dear Fr. McNulty:
   Please excuse William from school on Monday, June 3rd. He had a 24-hour virus.
   Thank you.

Respectfully yours,
Mary J. Connors

   I read that note over and over again that next morning after the kiss in the car with Al and I couldn't find anything wrong with the grammar or spelling, but I wasn't exactly thrilled with the 24-hour virus business because McNulty—the Dean of Discipline who I know I already mentioned—doesn't think you're sick unless you have leprosy or the plague or terminal cancer or something like that, and I had used this 24-hour virus excuse on the one occasion that I actually went through this bullshit in the auditorium: last winter during a snowstorm. I remember because I had on these noisy boots which made a racket when I walked down the aisle and handed McNulty the note. You have to bring in a doctor's note or at least a note from your mother saying why you've been absent and he reads each one out loud and by the inflection and tone of his voice he'll actually insult your mother right in front of every-body. You never know when he'll get to you because the names aren't in alphabetical order or anything and once he's through with you you have to go and sit back down so that the audience doesn't dwindle as he goes through the names.

I stood there with my hands behind my back. He opened the note and read it and put his hands on his hips. They were on his waist just above his ass with his fingers pointed toward his asshole and his thumbs visible in front and his elbows arched back. He stuck his chin out about two inches away from my mouth and said something like, "So the big baby boy had a twenty-four-hour virus." Everybody laughed and my face turned red. "Did mommy treat you well?" In other words he actually expected a verbal response to this and no matter what you say in situations like that you just sink deeper.

"Yes," I said.

"Yes WHAT."

"Yes, Father." I'd practically choke or gag when I had to call these pricks "Father."

"Did mommy keep you tucked in bed all nice and snug?" Uproarious laughter. "Did she give you orange juice and tea and aspirin?" A real side splitter. Rolling in the aisles.

"No, Father."

"Oh no? But you just said . . ."

And on and on. I saw guys get treated a lot worse than this, but I could not stand being embarrassed and angry in front of all those hyenas. If someone somehow managed not to get embarrassed or at least appeared not to be embarrassed or if he smirked or something, then McNulty just slapped him across the face real hard a couple of times which is what happened with the next guy who was called. McNulty hauled off and walloped him in the jaw with the heel of his right hand and the kid's face went flying off to the right at about a 120-degree angle and McNulty massaged the carpals in his hand and tears started welling up in the kid's eyes. If you get smacked that hard it sort of shakes up the inside of your head and the tears just kind of uncontrollably seep out. Which is the absolute worst thing you could ever want to do in front of those jokers. I personally never got slapped by him under these circumstances. That only happened once—at a haircut inspection.

Being on the swim team didn't get you out of this bullshit routine either, although it did if you were on the football team which really pissed Mr. Bieniwicz off, so he stopped having practice on Mondays and Tuesdays. The trick if you were going to be absent on a Monday was to be absent the next day also because then you just handed the note in during homeroom as if you were only absent Tuesday and that's what I did ever since.

The last kid that day last winter was named Jose Villanueva and his note said, "Please to excuse Jose en Monday for that he sick." McNulty pronounced each word perfectly and distinctly right in front of everybody and they all doubled up in stitches which was exactly the desired effect because it made this kid Jose turn red and feel like a piece of shit. Jesus Christ would roll over in his grave if he knew pricks like this were priests.

I left for school at the usual time with the note and a blank piece of my mother's writing paper in one of my books and walked through the park to Pelham Bay station. Instead of getting on the subway I went into Ida's which is a candy store there where I waited for Vickie's Beauty Salon to open. Mr. Bieniwicz would have had a shitfit if he saw what I ate there—a chocolate egg cream, a pack of Devil Dogs, three long pretzels, four jelly royals and a vanilla egg cream—especially since the invitational was that coming Saturday.

I'm always amazed and amused whenever I see a truant officer on a TV show. I have never in my life laid eyes on such a thing as a truant officer and I've never met a single person who has. Dog catchers fall into this category also. I've just brought this up to make it clear that on days like this it was never necessary to lay low or hide out or anything like that. I'd just hang around Ida's and read the *Village Voice* or *Mad* magazine or *The New Republic* or something like that till 9:30 and then I'd go around the corner to Vickie's where my friend Emo works who forges my absence notes. She used to live across the street and down the block from us in a basement apartment that was filled with brand-new stolen clothes which her mother, Hot Phyllis, sold to all the neighbors at very cheap prices. They moved out very suddenly one day and no one knows what happened to Hot Phyllis and no one has seen her since, but Emo is now a beautician. That's not her real name and I've never seen it in print but it's pronounced EE-mo. She's very fat and everybody calls her Fat Emo, even right to her face, but I just call her Emo. Her real name is Minerva or Aurora or something like that. She wears a white beautician's outfit with ripped seams on the waist and ass and she usually has on these old pink plastic slippers with holes in them that her little toes stick out of and she smokes Eve cigarettes. She charges anyone else $5.00 for an absence note but she does mine for nothing because I hang around with her for a few hours and talk and go to Ida's and get her chocolate shakes or walkaways or magazines.

She was putting pink plastic rollers onto a bleached blond wig on a styrofoam head when I showed up. A cigarette was dangling out the side of her mouth and she was squinting from the smoke and I was telling her about Tommy and Lorraine and she said, "She's marryin' this guy and he's the only one she ever fucked?" Emo was about twenty and she didn't know Tommy or Lorraine.

I was sitting on a turquoise fiberglass chair with my legs crossed, smoking a Marlboro, being cool in my blue pinstripe suit. I hardly ever smoke but I do when I visit Emo at Vickie's. "I'm not absolutely positive he's the only one she's ever fucked, but they've been seeing each other since puberty practically so I don't see how she could have, although I guess it's possible that—" I caught a glimpse of myself in the mirror "—that one of them or both of them has fucked around on the side but I don't think so." My mouth always looks weird to me when I see myself in a mirror talking or exhaling smoke. I used to try to look at myself in our bathroom mirror and not have my eyes look back at me. Actually I still try to do that now and then even though I know it's not going to work. It's sort of the opposite of what happens when you're on a subway or something and you're reading a book or the paper and you're aware that someone across the aisle or someone standing in front of you is looking at you. The second you look up at them they look away and act like they weren't looking at you. Most people never seem to be aware of it when someone is staring at them but I always know when someone is staring at me even if I don't actually see them out of my peripheral vision. The way I slightly jumped—not jumped—the way I slightly froze each time I made eye contact with myself in Vickie's reminded me of something but I couldn't figure out what.

Emo said, "Well, I ain't gettin' married."

"How come?"

She took the cigarette out of her mouth. Exhaling, she said, "Who the fuck wants to get married?"

"People get married all the time. What are you talking about?"

"Well, I'm not gettin' married. No way." She put the cigarette in an ashtray and went back to the head.

"Why not?"

"What the fuck do I want to get married for?"

"Practically everybody gets married."

"Well, I wouldn't get married if you paid me."

That's the way these conversations with Emo go. Just when they don't seem to be headed anywhere we'll suddenly stop going around in circles and she'll say something that makes a lot of sense to me, like the next thing she said was, "Well, maybe if you paid me. I mean, I can see gettin' married for the money and the presents—and then get it annulled." Emo is one of the more intelligent people I know.

I caught myself in the mirror again and again I felt sort of déjà vu I guess you'd call it. I was thumbing through a movie magazine. There was something I wanted to talk to Emo about and several times I almost spit it out but I kept sort of gagging on the words every time I tried. She asked me what was bugging me. I stood up. "I'm going to Ida's and get you some new magazines.

These are the same ones you had last time. You want anything?"
"Coffee."

I had looked forward to spending a couple of hours with her but now that I was there I wished I was someplace else. I don't mean it was one of those ejector button situations. It was more like the feeling you get when you buy a record and you get it home and it skips.

When I got back from Ida's I said, "Do you like to have sex? With men?"

She was through with the head and was starting on another. I've hardly ever seen her doing a real head because I usually leave if any customers come in. She wasn't startled or anything by this question, which is what I like about her. "Yeah," she said. "Some men."

"Why?" I asked.

"Why what?"

"Why do you like to have sex with men?"

"Because it feels good. What do you think?"

"But what feels good about it?"

"What are you talkin' about? It feels *good*."

"You mean—to come, to have an orgasm?"

"Girls have orgasms too, you know."

"Is that what you like about it? Can't you—don't you do that by yourself?"

"You're gettin' all worked up, Billy. You got some kind of problem?"

"Don't you masturbate and—you know, think about guys while you're doing it?"

"Yeah, but that's different."

"Different from what?"

"Different from doing it with a man."

"Why?"

"Because you're with a *man*."

"What about it?"

"Because you're *with* somebody—someone's body—not just their body, their—it's *sex*. It feels *good*, what do you *want* from me?"

"You mean their bodies? You like the way a man's body feels all over you?"

"Yeah, of course." I plopped down into a chair and she said, "Ain't you ever had sex before?"

I thought about Sunday night with Lorraine and I said, "Yes—" which was technically the truth, but it was everybody else's truth, not mine "—and no."

"What the fuck does that mean?"

"I don't feel like going into it right now. I have to go anyway." People don't always want to hear everything you want to tell them. And anyway—and I think this is the main reason I didn't say what was on my mind—Emo is a girl. She was sexually attracted to men, so you might think that we had that in common, but it's not the same thing for a girl to be sexually attracted to a man as it is for a man. I had to talk to a man about it. My father was out of the question. And any other man I knew was also into women and at best wouldn't understand and at worst would call me a faggot and tear ass from the room, knocking over a few chairs on the way.

I went to the park with Emo's forged note in my pocket. By this time it was sunny but the ground was still wet from the storm the night before. I blotted some beads of water with my handkerchief off a bench and watched an old parky remove soggy trash from a water fountain that had been broken for at least a year. I sat on the bench and slumped down with my ankles crossed and my arms crossed and thought that there must be someone who I could tell all this to, and the thought occurred to me that I could probably talk to Mr. Bieniwicz maybe. Then I was watching two squirrels tearing ass up an acorn tree one after the other and it dawned on me that what it was in the mirror in Vickie's was the same way Al and I froze when our eyes met the day we first saw each other through the plate-glass window of the McCarthy headquarters. I didn't know what this meant. But I thought it was good. You never can tell if squirrels are playing or fighting or what.

CHAPTER

15

MY MOTHER'S VOICE FROM THE bathroom shattered whatever it was I was dreaming about. She walked past my room and yelled, "Billy! Time to get up!" through the closed door and went into their room where she does her hair and makeup at a blond vanity table backlit by morning sun.

I was flat on my stomach, not a muscle moving or willing to move except my cock, hard at digging a hole in the mattress. An arm was dead asleep in a contorted position under a saliva-soggy pillow. I cracked my eyes open. Spotting a few crumpled tissues on the floor, I rolled over onto one side, massaging the dead arm while my hard-on jumped and kicked. I'm not pointing these things out because they were unusual or anything. In fact so far it was a very regular typical morning. One reason it would always take me forever to get up is that at least until my mother's cab came I figured I couldn't waltz around the house with a boner bouncing through my Fruit of the Looms.

I rolled onto my back and right on schedule, in the way that things POP into your head as you're waking up in the morning, I thought about Hogan and as usual, it felt as if somebody was pressing a large thumb against my chest, caving my lungs in slightly, forcing a long slow sigh out through my nose as my cock surrendered and fell over dead. With another POP I remembered the California primary, got out of bed and headed for the TV in the living room, passing the kitchen where the back of my mother's head was silhouetted against the window. She was standing at the sink and between crunches of an English muffin she said to the window, "Your water's on." For freeze-dried coffee. The Broadway score to *Man of La Mancha* was playing on the stereo in the living room and my finger was on the reject button. I was about to ask if it was alright with her if I shut it off but I didn't. She either would have said "No, I'm listening to it" or else "Okay"—while sighing and shaking her head. So I left it alone and turned on the TV and stood there as the picture came into focus. When I went to bed the night before, Kennedy was leading by a hair but McCarthy wasn't conceding and the networks weren't calling it so I was still hopeful. The picture focused and there was Kennedy claiming victory at a podium that said Ambassador Hotel on it. It was a tape, a few hours old. Mrs. Kennedy had on a white sleeveless dress and her arms were very tan with saggy wrinkled triceps. My mother was also wearing a sleeveless dress that morning but without the sags and wrinkles. She's only thirty-four. Kennedy scratched himself above his eye and smiled. He left the podium and walked through a doorway, cheering people closing behind him. Another camera from a viewpoint beyond the doorway picked him up and now he was coming towards me down a hallway, smiling with teeth and reaching out, shaking hands. Jostled, he brushed his hair back with his hand and kept coming. The camera started jerking, then you couldn't see him and people started screaming and the camera jumped and swung and vaulted straight up to the ceiling to fluorescent lights and held there with muffled screams and something shot up my spine. The camera swept back down and down out of focus, in focus and then it was on him going down for a second, it jerked down and left and up and right and on him, his face a blank ashen mask for a moment, people screaming and the camera pitched to the right, back again and there he was on the floor, blood pouring out the back of his head through the fingers of some guy who for a moment looked up, his eyes met mine and held for a second, Kennedy's right arm jerked and around him legs shuffled and stumbled and people screamed and tripped in much confusion. My mother said something from the bathroom while *Man of La Mancha* was still playing on the stereo and the camera bobbed up and right to a scuffle that was going on and then back. No one looked like they knew what the hell to do other than hold his head and put their hands under it so that blood splashed through their fingers into a puddle on the floor, then Mrs. Kennedy arms flailing her mouth GET BACK GET BACK GIVE HIM ROOM GET BACK his eyes glazed and glazed with nothing to do, nothing for them to do when you're useless and helpless, you are very very lame. Even Walter Cronkite. "Robert Kennedy has been shot." My mother behind me ready for work, "What's the matter?! What happened?! Billy, honey, what's the matter!" Cronkite giving the hospital report. "Once again, Senator Robert Francis Kennedy has been critically wounded in an assassination attempt—"

"Oh, my God," my mother said and came over and put an arm around me and I stiffened solid and racked. She took her arm away. "Say something. Are you okay?" She stood there and I looked out the window. I wanted to call Al, I was afraid, didn't know what, didn't know shit.

When I was a kid riding this brand-new red Schwinn bike in the park that my parents gave me for my birthday, two older black kids stole it while I was getting a drink of water and I ran home crying my head off. My mother came out of the house yelling What happened What happened!—she didn't work when I was a kid so she was home—and I told her and we sat on the stoop where she rocked me back and forth holding my head against her and we both cried our heads off for a very long time like the world's worst disaster had just happened to us and I don't think she was crying about the bike.

A horn honked once from outside which was her cab but she didn't go. She remained behind me for a minute and said, "Are you okay, baby?"

"Your cab's outside," I said.

"The cab can wait, damn it, are you okay?"

"Yeah."

"Don't stand there too long. You have to get ready for school."

"So long," I said, and she left. When I heard the front door slam from the hall and through the window from outside, I watched her get in the cab and it drove away.

In the kitchen I drank some coffee that she had poured for me. It was lukewarm. I held the cup in my hand and examined a knot in the wooden cabinet door, entered the knot, floated down into it bouncing off the sides occasionally but mostly just floating down and down into it and it had no bottom and from the living room the same screams came that I heard a few minutes before again and again, screams for what I don't know I don't know who knows anything I don't know SHIT. It doesn't matter. It doesn't matter what order any of this is in.

Sometimes your emotions double triple on top of each other on account of the emotions themselves, like I was upset and shaky but I think it had to do with my being really surprised or shocked or something at the way I reacted to what I saw on the TV. In other words I was upset because I had gotten so upset. But also because I was mad at myself for shaking my mother's arm off. Kennedy also beat McCarthy in South Dakota that same day. Who cares.

Any doubts I might have still had about talking to Mr. Bieniwicz were gone for some reason, and on my way through the park to the station I decided to talk to him that day after practice.

On the subway all I saw was RFK SHOT! all over the place on all the *Daily News*es being read with the usual blank expressions on their faces and I'll tell you the truth, I didn't have the nerve or the heart to wear my McCarthy button that day.

It's not till that train gets to Hunt's Point that any black or Puerto Rican people get on and some of them were talking about it and shaking their heads and being quite miserable about it, and then this one fat black woman standing in front of me actually starts crying and wailing and moaning, "Martin! Bobby! Oh my Lord Jesus save us! Nobody left now! Oh, Bobby! Only Lord Jesus now!"

Mostly everybody was trying to act like nothing was going on and she was getting more and more upset so I got up and let her sit down and she was waving a hanky at her face and sobbing. The white man and the white woman to her right and left looked like they either wished she'd quit it or that they could continue acting like nothing was going on and still feel comfortable and natural about it. I'm not trying to set myself up as some kind of Good Samaritan or anything. Ordinarily you'd have to be dying or *very* old in order for me to actually get up and give you my seat, like those old ladies who have gotten so short they can't reach the handles. Some people make beelines to kids like me and stand in front of you and pretend they can just barely reach and moan and sigh and massage their hand when the train stops. Once I saw a guy drag himself onto the train limping real severely, worse than Tommy, and somebody gave him their seat and when the train landed at 125th Street he tore ass across the platform to the express like an Olympic sprinter. So I never give my seat to anybody hardly. This day was the exception in other words, even though for all I know that fat black woman could have been faking the whole scene just to get the seat, but I'm sure she wasn't. I think I can tell the difference.

Right where you get off the subway there's this Greek coffee shop, this greasy spoon, where I'd have breakfast every day a half hour before school with Joey. He'd get on at the very next stop after mine but we wouldn't bother trying to meet up with each other until we were all the way there. It's not really a Greek restaurant—I mean it's run by Greeks and you can get a feta cheese omelet or a feta cheeseburger and the name of the place is Mykonos but we just called it the Spoon. It's very long and narrow with booths along one wall and a long counter running down the other wall. Joey was a junior and we didn't have any classes together and I hardly ever ran into him, so those mornings with him at the Spoon were the only connection between my real life and my school life and it always felt weird—like when you stand on the middle of a seesaw and balance it back and forth with your feet up and down, not letting the ends touch the ground.

You're not allowed to smoke within a five-block radius of Hogan, believe it or not, and if an S.C. spots you they actually report you and you get detention. The Spoon was about six feet outside the heat zone so it was crammed every morning with wild and hollering Hogan students smoking their brains out drinking coffee. There was a cashier up front and behind this long counter were about five countermen, evenly spaced. Each morning Joey and I would sit at the very last station in the back and chitchat with Tony, the counterman there who was a very old guy who usually got your order wrong. The place was always so crowded it would have been no problem sneaking out and not paying at all, but each day we'd alternate. We'd get separate checks and slip one into a pocket or a book as we shoved our way up front to the cashier. Nobody ever found out.

There was Joey outside the Spoon that day wearing his usual morning sunglasses. "What the hell you been doin' the last two days?" he wanted to know.

I shrugged and mumbled something about McCarthy. While we were elbowing our way through the mob to the back to wait for two stools in Tony's station, Joey shouted over his shoulder, "You heard about Tommy and Lorraine, right?"

We got two seats right away. "What about them?" I said.

"Shit, you ready for this?" He unbuttoned his shirt at his navel, leaned over toward me and while lighting a Silva Thin cigarette said, "They eloped and took off to California yesterday."

"*What?*" I right away pictured Tommy emptying his father's .45 into Bobby Kennedy's head, which struck me as both possible and out of the question. "Are you kidding?" I said. You never knew with Tommy.

"Naw'm not kidding," Joey said.

"How'd they get there?"

"I dunno. Bus, I guess." In that case they were still on their way, and anyway they had arrested some Arab right on the spot.

Tony put two cups of coffee in front of us and said, "Morning, professors." He always called us that and he amused himself whenever he said it. "At's shame, at's terrible, Mr. Kennedy, hah?"

"Yeah, I know," I said as Joey emptied sugar packets into his coffee. "You hear anything new about it?" I asked. "Like is he dead yet?"

"Naw, naw. I don't hear nothing here," Tony said, waving his hand through the smoke and noise.

"I'll have the usual, Tony." This was Joey. His usual was always different but that didn't matter to him. I said I'd just have a chocolate donut.

Joey said, "You're not hungry?"

"No."

"At least it wasn't your man. You still involved with that shit, huh?"

I nodded.

"—Whatsa matter?"

"I have a stomachache." What I really had was that thumb-pressed-on-the-chest feeling as I remembered the phone call I had with Lorraine Monday night. "Who told you about Tommy and Lorraine?"

"Do you believe that shit? Like somethin' out of an old movie, I dunno. Who the fuck *elopes*? His mother calls me last night, right? All hysterical, right? Tells me they eloped'n all. She thought I was his best friend or some shit."

That night in the park Lorraine said she wanted to elope with me and move to California. And she wanted to tell me something or ask me something on the phone at the end there the other night, but I was too annoyed over the whole Sue business to listen to her.

"You're acting pretty weird," Joey said.

Kennedy, Bieniwicz and Lorraine were all jumping around inside, making me feel lousy or nervous for all different reasons. Tony put the food in front of us. Joey's usual that day was bacon and eggs over easy with a corn muffin and I got a cinnamon donut, sliced. I ate half of it and gave Joey the other half. He dunked it in his coffee and held it dripping. "I don't know what you're all weirded out about. There's nothing you can do about it, right? So don't sweat it. It's a drag, I know." He took a bite of the donut. "That Tommy was a real turd."

I never really believed Lorraine loved Tommy even though I'd constantly tell her she did all the time whenever they had an argument just to smooth things out, to make peace, for Tommy's sake more than hers I now realize. He would have been lost without Lorraine. Then it dawned on me that maybe he actually forced her at gunpoint to split with him, even if he didn't shoot Kennedy.

Joey nudged me. "Hey! Earth to Connors—"

"Huh?"

"I heard that you and, uh—what's her name? Sue?"

"Yeah."

"Broke up."

"Yeah."

"You did?"

"Uh huh."

"I can't figure you sometimes, Billy. What a fuckin' fox she was."

I didn't say anything.

He was smearing grape jelly on the last bit of corn muffin. "Well, it's her loss, right?"

"Right."

"You being such a great conversationist 'n all."

Gradually over the course of the day Kennedy got put further and further into a corner of my brain as my talk with Mr. Bieniwicz got closer and closer. After practice I took my sweet time combing my hair a million times, till I was the last one left and then I went into the battleship where he was the only one there, dressed in slacks and a shirt this time, staring at a small transistor radio on the desk that I don't think I ever noticed there before. He was holding a ballpoint pen suspended over an open notebook. There was a news report on about Kennedy.

I stood in the doorway and made some kind of noise with my foot or a book or something and he looked up and looked at me and said, "What's up, Connors?" with his pen still poised over the notebook as if he thought whatever it was I wanted would take about two seconds.

I said, "Uh, can I, uh, well—I wanted to, do you have a minute, a few minutes?"

"Well—yes." He sat up straight and started clicking the pen.

"Is he dead yet?" I asked.

"No. Just a vegetable." He shook his head. "I can't believe it." He stared at the desk for a second, then shut off the radio and said, "What's up?"

I went and sat down in the chair next to the desk but I didn't like the arrangement. "I wanted to ask you something—ask you about something and uh, it doesn't have anything to do with the team or anything."

He put the pen down. He kept looking at me, waiting, not impatiently, with this slightly startled look on his face, like I had come in there with my shirt on backwards or something.

"Maybe we can go outside," I said. "If that's okay—like on the field."

He got right up and as we walked outside in silence to the deserted practice field I felt kind of stupid. We sat on a bench, both on the edge of it.

"What's the story?" he asked.

"You're not going to believe this." I was cracking the knuckles in my toes. "I mean, I think you're going to be really shocked but I have to talk to someone, to a man, and you're the only one I know who I think won't be grossed out or shocked so you really ought to sort of decide before I go into it at all if you want to hear anything that might really bother you or shock you or annoy—"

"I'm listening, okay? I don't think I'll be shocked."

"I mean, I think you'd be less shocked if I told you I murdered someone or raped someone because this is something that everyone thinks is disgusting and perverted even though I don't, I think it's absolutely natural because it feels fine, it's the way my body feels, I like the way it feels—"

"Are you saying you're homosexual?"

"What?"

"Are you homosexual?"

"Uh, well—"

"Do you like other guys—sexually?"

"Yeah."

"Haven't you ever heard the word homosexual before?"

"*Of course* I've heard the *word*, it just sounds so stupid."

"Look, relax. What do you think it means?"

"I know what it means, but everyone else thinks it's men who wish they were women. Like the ones who wear dresses and makeup and hang around Greenwich Village."

He chuckled slightly and looked down at the turf. Then he looked at me. "Anyway, look—being—attracted to guys—it's a problem for you, I guess?"

"Well, yeah. Well, it wouldn't be a problem if everybody else didn't think it was a problem."

"There are certain conceptions about what's normal or acceptable, and in regard to your—sexuality, you don't meet society's acceptable—you go against the accepted norm."

"That doesn't mean they're right and I'm wrong."

"No . . . no, but you're going to have a tough time if you want to be able to be—"

"It's not what I *want* to be, like a—a fireman or a president of the United States, it's what I am. I've always been. I mean, I don't *not* want it but it's not like I made some kind of choice. Like, I didn't decide to have blond hair."

"It will be hard for you to func—to live the way you are, is what I'm saying. Most of society rejects homosexuality."

"There shouldn't even be words for these things," I said.

It was dusk and the sun was sinking behind grungy tenements beyond the practice field. The sky looked nice if you lifted your hand and covered the buildings.

I said, "I appreciate you taking the time—"

"Don't worry about it. Do you like girls at all, or what?"

"No. N. O. I mean, I *like* them, I have girl friends, you know, female friends. But, like—you know when guys talk about eating out cunt and stuff like that?" He nodded. "Well, the thought of it makes me puke."

"Have you ever had sex with a girl?"

"Well, yeah, sort of, once, I guess."

"What was it like?"

"I don't know. Like having sex with a pillow or I don't know what, just something I don't, something my body doesn't want to do. And I'm not going to keep forcing myself to do it just because—I mean if a guy who's not attracted to guys made out with a guy or a girl who wasn't attracted to girls made out with a girl— I'm talking tongues and everything—they'd barf. It's the same thing, and I'm not going to keep doing it just because everybody else says it's terrific and normal."

"Have you had sex with a guy?"

"No. Well, that's—see, that's sort of really what I specifically what I wanted to talk to you about."

"Yeah." He started clicking that ballpoint pen which he brought out there with him.

"I think I'm going to have sex with a guy on Saturday night— after the invitational."

"You mean it's all planned?"

"Yeah, it's planned, it's sort of a date, I guess. He's coming to the meet and everything." I told him about Al's parents going away for the weekend and everything.

Now he was fingering his whistle and looking down at the turf and I plowed on. I told him quite a bit about Al and blushed a lot. "And we actually kissed once and I don't mean a peck on the cheek and I jerk off all the time to him but I'm not sure—I don't really know what to do."

"Have you gone to—have you thought about seeing the school psychologist?"

I looked at him with my hands dangling between my legs and my mouth sort of dropped open and I said, "Huh?"

"Or some other psychologist or therapist of some sort—I don't really know if going to the school psychologist would be the best idea—having all this written down on your record."

I was turning red and the hairs on the back of my neck were standing up. "What are you talking about?" I said.

"I mean, there are—I figured you didn't realize this—there are supposedly, from what I understand, ways of changing, through psychotherapy or—"

"Oh. Right." I stood up. "Well, thanks a lot for taking the time. I gotta go now." And I split. I didn't look back, so I don't know if he got up or remained sitting there or what.

CHAPTER

16

ON THE TRAIN I WAS KIND OF NUMB, feeling like a total jerk for talking to Mr. Bieniwicz. Sometimes when you look back on things you've done you have absolutely no idea why you did them—what you had in mind at the time, what you thought you were doing the thing for. When I said to him, "I don't really know what to do," I didn't mean what to do about getting "*cured*," like some cancerous growth or something that there's no reason on earth you'd want it. I meant what to do specifically, sexually, with *Al*, like how to suck a cock or how to have your ass fucked—no, not how to have your ass fucked, I had not yet even *heard* of that. Not that I was looking for exact answers to these things from Mr. Bieniwicz, but—well, now I don't know what the hell I was looking for. And homosexual. A great word. Like Hitler or communism, words that gross people out or make them shudder.

I tried to put all this out of my mind by browsing through the back of my ancient history notebook where I think I mentioned I've got Al's name written all over the place, and even his initials and my initials inside of hearts that you're supposed to carve on trees. One thing girls do all the time is to write their name as though they were married to some guy, like "Mrs. Joe Schmo." There on the subway, in the book, I wrote "Mr. Al DiCicco." But then I said no, that would still be him, not me. Then I realized that it was both, if you see what I mean: him and me. Because if I was to, like, marry him, I'd still be Mr. Bill Connors but I'd also become Mr. Al DiCicco and he'd still be Mr. Al DiCicco but he'd become Mr. Bill Connors, see? We would be both of us. And I thought that was quite great even if you think it was corny or stupid because I know men can't get married.

I closed the book and crossed my legs and closed my eyes and thought about Al's hands and mouth. I couldn't wait to meet him at the McCarthy office although I didn't really feel like canvassing while this business with Kennedy was going on. All of a sudden the picture of Kennedy's blood pouring out the back of his head jumped into my head and I right away felt bad for forgetting about Kennedy because as every well-trained Catholic knows—even those who don't actually believe any of it—when you've got something to be happy about on the one hand and on the other hand you've got something to feel miserable about, you pick the miserable one. That's to make you a better person and that way you'll do less time in purgatory. You figure it out. It doesn't make any sense to me but if you've been brainwashed about something from the day you're born, you sometimes act that way even after you're old enough to see that it's all a load of shit.

Walking down Crosby Avenue after getting off the subway, I could see people in front of the McCarthy office down the block, including Al, standing around with their arms folded, talking low in small groups. A lot of those volunteers hardly ever did anything other than stand around talking with their arms folded anyway, but the shooting gave them a good excuse.

Al saw me coming and he hopped and broke away from them. He's a little shorter than me even though he's four years older, and slightly bow-legged. When he walks he leans forward a bit and even when he's standing still. Going towards each other was as though our movement was being aided by the other, made easier, like on a moving sidewalk at the airport. We stopped short, about a foot from each other, and didn't do anything physical like putting our arms around each other which is what we wanted to do. He asked me where I was when I found out about Kennedy and I told him and I even told him I cried but I didn't say anything about sinking down into the wooden knot in the kitchen cabinet. He told me he was in his car, already on his way to school.

The last time I had seen him was Monday, the night we made out in his car. He didn't feel like doing any canvassing either. I asked him what he felt like doing. He moved his eyes down my body and then up at me, smiling with his teeth. Then he went, "Ahem." We both sort of laughed, with our hands in our pockets.

He said, "How about going up to Nathan's?" In Tuckahoe.

"Okay." Nathan's is this huge place with a million pinball machines and they sell all kinds of food. I had been there many times before with Joey and Roxanne.

"We could take the Sprain," he said. "It's got no lights on it." Joey always took the Thruway.

So we rode up the Sprain Brook Parkway which is dark and

twisty and we blared the radio on the way. I wanted to tell him about what happened with Mr. Bieniwicz but I didn't. We weren't ready to actually talk about things like that. In fact, I never told him about it.

He told me he had been talking to a friend of his, a schoolmate who was getting credit for campaign work for the Regular Democratic organization, the Uncommitteds. "He's getting a full-time summer job with them and he says he could probably get me one too." He said this staring straight ahead with both hands on the wheel, which you may say is not so unusual when you're driving a car, but ordinarily he would drive with one hand and look over at me or glance over a lot while he's talking and touch me and stuff like that.

I asked him if the Uncommitteds were still uncommitted.

"Well, you know—yeah. Technically."

"They're really for Humphrey, I'll bet." To me, Humphrey meant more of the War. And the Draft.

"Well, maybe Humphrey. Probably, but maybe not." He was gesturing with one hand on and off the wheel, still looking out straight. "They'll probably stay uncommitted right up to the convention. You know—bargaining power—leverage."

"Yeah."

"So it'll be great because I do need a summer job," he said. "But it's all still up in the air."

I asked him when he'd know and he said he was supposed to see some man about it the following week. I didn't like the way any of this sounded but I didn't know why.

"Why don't you light a joint," he said.

I took one out of the glove compartment, lit it, passed it to him and said, "So you'll know about the job before the primary, right?"

"Yeah, I guess so."

"Would you still work for McCarthy till then?"

"I don't think so."

"You said you weren't in this just for the credit you were get—"

"This could be a stepping-stone for my political career. The

McCarthy people will be gone in that bus the day after the primary. These Regulars have been around since the thirties," he said. "They're powerful people—and at least they're not Republicans." He passed me the joint but I didn't want it.

He placed it on the lip of the ashtray. "Let's not talk about this," he said.

He kept turning to look at me but I wouldn't look at him. "You know," he said after a while, "I'm really looking forward to Saturday night."

I knew what he meant but I said, "You mean the invitational?"

"Oh—that too." He leaned over while driving and took my chin and kissed me. I wanted to grab him right there.

At Nathan's we played pinball and used the opportunity to stand real close to each other, as if one was just watching the other, and press our legs and arms against the other. We ate fried clams and french fries and bought a pound of cookies in the bakery there and ate them in the car on the way back while we smoked another joint and we held hands whenever he didn't have to shift and even kissed occasionally, licking crumbs off each other's mouths.

I said, "I know this secret hidden road by the Pell Mansion."

He paused and then said, "Yeah?"

"We could go there for a while."

"What do you mean?"

"We could go there and, you know, park the car and—"

"You mean,—*park?*" He said this word "park" like it had quotes around it.

"Yeah."

"That road's no secret. Couples go there all the time. Boy and girl couples."

"No one's gonna stare into the car and see what we are."

"It's ridiculous. It's too risky."

I didn't say anything. I just sort of slumped down in the seat.

"How do you know about that road, anyway?" he wanted to know.

"My friend Joey told me about it."

"You went there with another *guy?*"

"I went there with this guy Joey and his *girl*friend. I mean, we didn't drive *in*. We were on the way to an Iona dance and he just slowed down there and pointed it out to me—"

"Why did he point it out to you?"

"He was just showing me where he goes all the time with his girlfriend Roxanne."

We were kind of yelling.

Where the Sprain meets the Thruway he got off and took the Thruway home. We didn't say anything. I was mad. Not because he wouldn't go park by the Pell Mansion but because he thought the idea stunk so much—plus I felt like he had been grilling me. Finally when we were getting near my house he took my hand and said he was sorry. After a few seconds I said, "It's okay."

In front of the bathroom mirror that night, standing in the tub, I mouthed the following words in a very exaggerated way without saying them out loud. "You. Are. A. Ho-mo-sex-u-al." On the last syllable, my tongue wound up touching my upper lip and I held it there. Staring into the mirror, I ran my tongue over my upper lip, very slowly, and then the lower one. I tried to picture Al saying and doing that in front of a bathroom mirror, and I couldn't.

The next day after Kennedy died, a lot of those people who get on the subway at Hunt's Point were suddenly wearing RFK buttons with black ribbons and so were a lot of students and teachers and people on the street everywhere. Walking toward Hogan with Joey amid the throng from the subway and the Spoon I saw that the flag in front of school was at half-mast which made me mad. Entering the building, I heard some kids laughing at the stupidity of putting the flag at half-staff for that commie queer Kennedy. Everybody who wasn't a total asshole was a queer. By the lockers, some other kid was asking somebody why the flag was at half-staff. It's not that he didn't think it should be, it's that he didn't even know that Kennedy had been killed, or if he did, he didn't really know who he was. This flag at half-staff was a lie in other words, if you ask me. People use the word hypocrisy but the word lie is easier and more accurate.

CHAPTER 17

OTHER THAN SOME GIRL TIME-keepers at this end of the pool, Al was the only one there so far, sitting aways down in the top back row of the bleachers under our gold-on-blue HOGAN banner, leaning forward with his forearms on his thighs and his hands clasped, looking across the pool at the huge saggy white-on-maroon MOUNT ST. MATTHEW banner with tassels and things on it. This was Saturday night, the big Bronx–Westchester invitational at the Mount that I've mentioned a million times but I don't know if I really feel like going into it because it was a huge drag.

There were six other banners scattered around, among them Kathy's—FARRELL—which is the lamest team on earth because they've only had boys in that school for a couple of years although they do have really attractive swimsuits with orange and yellow diagonal stripes. Every now and then Al would scratch his face or sit back and fold his arms or cross his legs. I figured he must have felt pretty weird sitting there behind the Hogan bench. After all, he swam on the Mount team and everything, so I bopped out from the locker room in just my swimsuit past those timekeepers, some of whose eyes followed me over to Al. He sat up straight and scanned my body, sort of like browsing, and like he was overcome by the experience, shook his head once and said, "Whew," as I plopped down next to him and said, "Hi."

"Hey, hotstuff," he whispered huskily, touching my arm with an elbow. "Excited about the meet?"

"Yeah." I was more excited about being with him later at his house.

He said, "I can't wait till later."

"Me neither."

He glanced around, scratching his neck, his mouth in an O. Back to me, a pucker and an airy kiss. I returned it.

He examined the palm of his hand. "Nice legs you got there, handsome."

"Quit it, will ya?" I pulled my legs together. "Shit."

He leaned back, laughing, his feet off the floor. If I had pulled down my suit I would have BOIINNGGGed straight out of it, in other words. And most of those timekeepers were watching us now, pencils or stopwatches in their hands.

"What am I gonna do?" I said, amused but getting worried. He responded with a laugh and I clipped him on the arm. He laughed harder and then so did I.

I stood and faced the wall and, pretending to be adjusting the Hogan banner, tried to think about Brother Laughlin drawing geometry all over a blackboard, but the left-hand gold vertical stripe of my suit was now pulsating, getting the stretch test of its life. "What the fuck am I gonna do? I have to go right by those girls."

"Dive in the pool," Al said. Which did the trick. I surfaced and boosted myself out and as I strolled past those girls I snapped the seat of my suit and said hi and a few of them smiled or giggled or said hi and one of them mumbled something about "snot nose." Before entering the locker room I tossed one last glance at Al and he beamed, a white flash. In a while the place got noisy with relatives and friends and students and so forth and there was Al alone among them.

*   *   *

"Judges and timers read-yy. Swimmers take your mark!"

It was my event, the 100-breast—a cinch. I stood on the block in lane four. Al was leaning on his hand, his elbow on his knee, watching me, happy and proud. He winked. The Kathy in lane five giggled. I don't know if he caught the wink or not, but Al had been doing it all night, each time I'd glance over to him, which was quite often.

The Iona Preppy in lane three false-started so we had to do it over. Al was now waving or signaling to someone across the pool, which threw me slightly as the gun went off, but I dove perfectly. I pumped and breathed and went and went and turning on their slippery wall was no problem. Turning again, into the third lap, I had a good lead. Then I looked. Which is one of the mortal sins of swimming. Looking. Ordinarily this means glancing to your right or left to see where the other swimmers are, and that slight split-second lapse can cost you the event, so it's something you *don't do*. But I not only looked, I looked *up* and *out* to the right into the bleachers for Al and he wasn't even there. So I fell behind and, looking out to the left for a split-second, saw him squeezing in next to some guy behind the Mount bench, the guy with his hand out for a shake. By now I must have dropped three seconds, completely blowing my lead. Mr. Bieniwicz was running alongside the pool yelling things at me. I was all pissed off and shaken up right there in the pool. I tried to make up for the lost time with the strength you use to punch a wall when you're mad. I surged and reached and stretched and forgot about their goddamn tile walls and slipped as I pushed off and in the end got touched out by the guy in lane five, who at that moment for some reason I thought was a Mountie. As I boosted myself out I couldn't look at anybody and then I remembered that it was that Kathy who was in lane five, not a Mountie, and there he was gloating in his orange-and-yellow suit, flexing his thighs over the fact that he came in *third*—Mount first and me *fourth*.

Mr. Bieniwicz ran over and hustled me over to the side. "What the hell were you looking at?" he said with this intense whisper which was more shock than anger. We were attracting a crowd, the rest of the Hogan team.

I was staring at my feet, thinking. Then I looked at him. "Nothing," I said.

His whistle was all jittery. "I don't understand."

"I shouldn't have looked, I know, I'm sorry, I shouldn't have been looking." I pulled away from him and broke between a couple of teammates and looked across the pool at Al—standing behind the Mount team—staring at me confusedly, his hands in his back pockets.

Then who bops over to me, blocking my sight line, but the Kathy who touched me out. "Hey, queer," he says, and giggles in this high-pitched manner.

"*What?*" I said.

He goes, "I hear you don't like girls, and you suck everybody off in the shower, that you—*OOOMPH*—" He doubled over, my fist in his stomach. I guess he wasn't expecting this from a faggot. Then I got grabbed and held from behind and so did he and he's yelling Faggot and Queer and Fuckin' homo and things like that and this big Hogan vs. Farrell shouting match erupted and all the coaches were keeping the two teams separated, trying to cool everyone down. Evan and Kevin surrounded me against a wall, saying things like, "Okay, relax, cool it," and stuff like that, their hands gripping my biceps. Mr. Bieniwicz ran over and Kevin said, "He's okay." I was looking at his chipped tooth.

I didn't get disqualified or anything. In the other events I used that fist-through-the-wall energy and we won the 100-medley and something else, I don't remember what. Winning that 100-breast meant more to me than I thought it could. If I hadn't looked I would have won and *then* seen that Al wasn't on the Hogan side, seen him on the Mount side reminiscing or some shit with some jerk ex-classmate. So it all would have turned out the same anyway but at least I would have won the 100-breast.

As a precaution they kept the Farrell team in by the pool till we were done in the locker room. I changed in a shaky daze without showering. I wanted to get the hell out of there. Everybody on the team was looking at me odd and I started to get embarrassed. You have to think in order to be embarrassed—think about what others are thinking and saying about you—and up until then I was just in this raw selfish state. Maybe it's sort of the way Sue felt when Lorraine and I dropped her off from the cab after Tommy's party and the screen door slammed. I don't know.

Mr. Bieniwicz breezed by in a big hurry and, grabbing onto the corner of a locker, said, "See me before you leave, okay?" which I didn't. On my way up the stairs Evan and Kevin overtook me with just their towels wrapped around them, their hair damp and mussed up. My head was even with their chests and they each had one erect nipple, one left and one right.

I said, "Listen, I'm really sorry about fucking up—"

"You have a lift?" asked Kevin.

I hesitated. "Yeah."

"With that guy?" asked Evan.

Those two were spooky, I swear. I was about to say "What guy?" but I found that I couldn't or didn't have to lie to them. I looked from one to the other and they sort of shifted or twitched their overbites. I said, "Your cowlicks just waved in unison."

They grinned at each other, communicating an unspoken thought—something they seemed to have already discussed.

I said, "Uh, so I'll see you guys next week, okay?" At finals.

"Okay," they said and I went around them up the stairs and I didn't look back.

Outside there was Al standing alone, leaning forward chewing gum, waiting for me with his thumbs in his belt loops. Our eyes connected and I stopped. He waited a second, then came over to me. "What's the matter?"

I walked away from him, looking at the ground, taking long strides toward the parking lot.

"Hey, wait up!" he said, trotting up next to me, taking hold of my arm. *"What's the matter?"* I yanked it free. "Nothing," I said, and kept walking. He grabbed it again and said, "Hold it, Bill."

I tried to jerk free but his grip was too strong. He grabbed my other arm. Facing him, I tried to break away. "Let go o' me!"

"Stop it," he said, pushing me against a car. I shoved him back hard, saying, *"Don't shove me, you fuckin' chickenshit!"* I tore out over a dark baseball field adjacent to the parking lot, not as fast as I could because he caught up to me and pinned my shoulders against a very huge acorn tree beyond left field.

"What the fuck is the matter with you?" he said, leaning his face in toward mine, holding me firm, his forehead moist with wet black curls.

"Go find your jerk Mount buddy," I said.

He turned his head for a second and spit the gum out into the air real forcefully like he was mad at it, piercing the dome of mist that enveloped the tree. Back to me, his pupils shifted in the dark, penetrating one of my eyes and then the other. Blue filtered yellow light from the parking lot glinted off two beads of sweat that rolled down from a sideburn, one faster than the other.

"I thought you came to this thing for me," I said. "To see me."

"I did."

"So then why'd you go over there by the Mount?"

"That guy was on my team in high school and he kept calling me over there. His brother is on—"

"So *what?*"

"You're making a big deal over nothing."

"I am *not*. I lost the event. You *made* me lose—"

"No I didn't." He let go of my shoulders. "You shouldn't have looked."

"You weren't even watching me."

"I was too."

"That was my big event and you're over there bullshittin' with some—"

"He was doing all the talking. I was watching you."

"No you weren't," I said, but I believed him. I looked down at the roots of the tree. "Oh shit," and I kicked at one of the roots, realizing how shrill I must have sounded. Looking down at our feet, I said, "So what did you say to him? Who'd you say I was?"

"I said you were my cousin."

My eyes started to well up so I opened them wide and looked up to one side and blinked so tears wouldn't seep out. My mouth started quivering though, and I felt a tear run out of one eye, hesitate on a cheekbone, then run down my face. My chest was heaving and I blinked and tried to stop but I couldn't. I slid down the tree without moving my feet and landed on my ass, my knees in the air. I cupped one hand over my eyes. Al took a step toward me. "Oh, Billy," he said, like a caress, but he didn't touch me. All you could hear was the occasional distant sound of a kid hollering or a car door slamming. I tried to speak but all I could get out was, "Wh . . . wha . . . what—" Finally I managed to say, "Why c-couldn't you just stay put and say that to him after—if you h-had to lie about it." From under my hand I watched his foot softly grinding acorns into the dirt.

"I don't know . . . I figured I could see you just as easy from over there. How was I supposed to know you were going to start gaping around for me in the middle of it." The parking lot was dead quiet now. The only sounds came from crickets in the tree. "Billy?" he whispered, still grinding the acorns.

"What?"

"I'm sorry."

"Oh, sure."

"I am." He lifted my chin. I pushed his hand away and blew my nose.

"Please don't push my hand away . . . Okay?"

I was picking at the bark of a root. He lifted my chin again and wiped my cheeks with a thumb. "I didn't know it was that important to you—my being there. I would have stayed put no matter what. I really mean it."

He looked around and then ran his hands slowly through my

hair. "You didn't get hurt in that fight, did you?"

"Some fight."

"That was some punch you landed, tough guy." He started to playfully spar with me, feinting and then jabbing at me, dancing around. "Hey! Tough guy!"

"Quit it," I said into my handkerchief as I blew my nose. "I'd like to know where that asshole got his information from."

"What?" he said, squatting in front of me, bouncing on his haunches.

"Nothing."

He looked around—like before, to make sure no one could see us—then leaned in slowly toward me, lifting his arms, aiming his palms at the tree, landing against it as he closed his eyes. He moistened his lips, not with his tongue but sort of by overlapping them. Then, in slow motion, he brushed his lips lightly back and forth and all around all over mine and I did the same. There was hardly any actual contact in other words but it sent volts up and out through my head. He pulled back slowly. I opened my eyes and saw stars, believe it or not. My head was about a foot off the tree and through the stars there was Al grinning and bouncing. I whispered hoarsely, "Why don't we go?"

"Okay," and he sprang up.

On our way back to the car I wished we had our arms around each other with our hands tucked under each other's rib cage, but I didn't think he'd go for that idea.

His was the only car left in the lot. But then, out of nowhere, a black Corvair convertible sped by. Its driver let out with a long high-pitched giggle and his passenger turned her head away from us, her long blond hair whipping in the breeze. I stopped and stared after the Corvair as it careened around a curve in the drive.

"That was Sue and that Kathy dipshit," I said.

"Who's Sue?" Al asked, unlocking the door.

"Oh. Some girl I went out with a few times."

He got in and reached over and unlocked my door. From the

glove compartment he removed this little leather pouch that he keeps joints in and said, "Well, I don't think they saw what we were doing."

I looked at him. "I don't give a shit if they saw us."

He held the unlit joint between his thumb and middle finger and as he carefully unfolded the ends, said to it, "That's how rumors get started, you know."

I ignored this. "It didn't even occur to me to look in the bleachers to see if she was there." He was lighting the joint. "She goes to Kathy's, see?"

"Mm." He shook out the match. "I thought you said you didn't have a girlfriend."

"She's not my girlfriend. I went out with her a couple of times on a double date to the movies." He passed the joint. "She's the dumbest girl I ever met. Dumber than I thought if she's going out with that turd."

Thumbing in the direction of the gate the Corvair went out, he said, "Oh, was that—"

"Yeah. I'm pretty naive, I guess."

He squeezed my thigh and I held his hand there. Then we took off.

When we got to his house we were both kind of nervous. We hadn't said too much in the car. The house was dead quiet. He kissed me on the mouth and he said he'd be right back and went back down the stairs. It was a two-family house, Al's family on the second floor, his grandparents—his mother's parents—on the first. I took off my windbreaker and sat down on a chair in the living room. The house smelled good—a sweet smell, sort of like sausages. The furniture was all pretty worn out with no plastic covers and the place needed a paint job—lots of kids' fingerprints on the archways where you grab on if you're allowed to do that. I wondered what the hell Al was doing. There were baby pictures and pictures of First Holy Communions and Confirmations and graduations all over the place—and a wedding picture—his sister, I guess. And four bronzed pairs of baby shoes on top of the TV. I got up and went over and looked at them and I wondered which ones were Al's.

In a minute he was back with a dusty bottle of red wine with no label on it. He held it up. "This is from my grandfather's wine cellar. You like wine?"

"Yeah, sort of," I said. Actually I'm not too crazy about it.

He went into the kitchen and came back with two glasses and a corkscrew and sat on the floor and took off his sneakers and socks and opened the bottle. I wanted to smell his feet. I like feet quite a lot—if they're real attractive like Al's: long and thin with a few black hairs on the arches which are high and bony and black hairs are on his ankles. I pictured his hairy legs. I sat down facing him, both of us Indian style, like in the Circle.

We just kind of looked at each other, smiling, and we drank the wine which was as strong as straight liquor. The red of the two glasses was the only color you could see with the lights out in that living room, everything else lit blue from the outside night through the window.

I took off my sneakers and socks and dumped them with Al's and I liked the way they looked there thrown together. We let our bare feet touch. He pulled his polo shirt off over his head and said, "Why don't you take your shirt off, handsome?"

As I unbuttoned it he shook his head and ran his fingers through his black curls. A vein stood out on each arm and ran down from his shoulders through his biceps. A thin line of fine black hair ran up from below his navel to his chest where it kind of spread out and disappeared. He reached both hands out and ran his fingers along my arms, then he shifted and squatted and went to stand up and sort of tugged on my hands for me to stand up too. We stood there for the longest time with our pants on, shirts off, barefoot, slowly feeling each other's chest and arms quite slowly and gradually with the butts of our hands, stepping on each other's feet, accidentally at first. I ran my fingers up the narrow line of hair that went up his belly. There were a few hairs below each nipple.

"I really like your body," I said.

He said, "I really like yours too." I hardly have any hair on my body.

He wrapped his hands around my waist and squeezed. His fingers almost met. He moved to the obliques and I ran along the raised veins on his forearms. I reached up under his arms and squeezed his lats. He put his hand on my shoulder and, standing on my feet, kissed me on the mouth. Glued together, we toppled onto the floor. On top of him, pressing the base of my cock through my pants against him and then we'd roll over and switch, all around, pushing and pressing like wrestling, like fighting practically at times, then this would calm down and we'd lay there with a knee shoved up under a crotch with the knee kind of massaging the hard cord that runs from the ass to the base of the cock and great stuff like that. Our eyes inches away diving in and he looked and I looked and we were smiling and laughing a lot and we kissed and kissed, open-mouthed, and it all came very natural.

We were taking a breather and had some more wine and I said, "Al?"

"Huh?" he said as he tipped the wine away from his mouth.

"You ever do this before?"

"You mean—this?"

"Yeah."

"Not really."

"What do you mean?"

"Well, there was this kid down the block who moved upstate, and we used to give each other blowjobs but—" He shrugged and sipped some more wine. "That wasn't the way we are."

"What do you—"

"I mean, I don't even think I liked him." He put his hand behind my neck and massaged. "Why do you want to talk about that now?"

"Oh, I don't really, it's just—I don't really know how experienced you are and, like—"

He laughed. "What do you think, I'm gonna force you to do anything?"

"No—"

"C'mere."

The pants came off to just briefs and we felt each other through the white cotton. His were BVDs which are slightly different than Fruit of the Looms. Then they came off and he went down on me, went wild on it very expertly but I pulled out even though it felt *great* because I could have popped right then.

I wondered how he could do it without choking because I wanted to do the same to him but I wanted to do it right. He sat against the couch with his cock bouncing at my face with a little bit of goo on the slit. I swallowed just the head and it tasted great and felt great in my mouth and it smelled great down there but he said, "Careful of the teeth," and I tried again.

He lifted my head. "Like this," he said, demonstrating—opening his mouth wide and stretching his lips around his teeth. I tried it and I did it okay but I kept gagging as I tried to go down further. He said, "It's okay, you'll get it, it's all muscle control."

We did the famous 69 that I was looking forward to but I liked doing it separate better.

Anyway, I won't go into all the details but I couldn't believe it was happening and the *taste* and *smell* I really can't describe and then we were face to face horizontally and melded together—sweaty, locked legs, arms entwined, all muscles alert, sticky cocks smashing together and wet sweat.

Right before I came it was like suspended animation forever deep inside. Bodies clamped with arms and legs in vise holds, mouths locked, trying to get inside each other, the underbase of my tongue sore from stretching it down his throat, we hollered into each other as we came and came.

Then it was good and bad. Bad when the memory entered my

head of looking while swimming and seeing Al with the Mount team. From two inches away he whispered, "What's the matter?" "Nothing," I said. We laid there squished suctioned together, me trying not to think of anything, massaging lats, deltoids and everything. Then he started like munching on my ear and sticking his tongue in there which I didn't like and we started sucking real slowly on each other's lips and we'd fall asleep and wake up simultaneously, startled, and go at it for the longest time and fall asleep and—well, this went on for hours. All night, actually. The next day my lips were all swollen puffy like somebody had punched me in the mouth practically.

I was awake facing a window. We were in his bed in his room which I didn't even remember going in there. The position we were in was like two broken-in baseball gloves, me tucked inside the other one. Early-morning light was trying to get in and around the sides and bottom of the blinds, and shapes on the curtains were becoming dogs and hunters, the dogs much bigger than the hunters like the hunters were away in the distance and couldn't catch up and the dogs didn't feel like waiting for them. The window was shut and the room was musty thick and it smelled good.

I was on my left side, Al's bottom leg aligned along mine, his right arm slung over me, his palm up, limp in front of my face, his fingers curled back, twitching now and then. I looked at the wide white fingernails and down at his thigh which was clamped over me—the way you curl up on the floor with pillows shoved between your legs and watch TV for instance.

I reached back, trying not to wake him, and felt along his rump which was smooth and solid. I grazed over the hairs on his thigh. He burped, a small one, like you wouldn't have heard it six feet away. His knee came up toward me so his thigh was now nestled in right below my ribcage. I tucked my hand in under there above the back of his knee and held on. The next thing I remember was waking up again still like that, broad daylight now breaking in and around the blinds which were shut black. Birds and cars and kids' voices made their way in. My back was sore and I had a slight headache. Al's mouth was open, wet on my neck, breathing, not really snoring. Occasionally he'd burp or sniff or something. I adjusted my breathing and we rose and fell, the mattress giving like we were a solid weight. My stomach and his stomach were both growling and I couldn't tell which one it was that was growling—from hunger but I didn't even want food, I just wanted to stay there. I tried to go back to sleep and even though I couldn't I didn't want Al to wake up because I figured that would mean getting up and getting dressed and everything. I felt him swelling against my ass. I shifted so he could slip it between my legs, right along my cord which was now also hard. I squeezed tight there with my adductors—the inner thigh muscles. I uncurled his fingers, and with the pads on the tips of my fingers aligned against his, I pressed down against his hand and flexed, like on a mirror. My fingers moved down, touching the dry healed calluses on his palm right below each finger. His fingers enclosed my hand. I interlocked my fingers through his and in his sleep he did the same and he pulled my hand in against my chest. Between my legs he was now butting at one of my balls. I relaxed my thighs and shifted and pushed back and the head of his dick poked through. It was a different color than mine—like medium rare—something I hadn't noticed in the night, the color of his lips.

Our stomachs were both making a racket. All of a sudden he's giving me these little kisses on the back of my neck and shoulders and all around there. Then he whispered with a thick morning voice, "Hi baby." It felt kind of weird being called *baby* but I liked the way he said it, although I didn't say it back to him. "Hi," I said, pointing straight out, waving at the window. He lifted his head and looked. He wrapped his fist around the base of it, rolling it back and forth. A bit of goo came out and he wiped it off with his finger and licked it. I thought of doing the same to him but I didn't feel like it. "Are you hungry?" I asked. "Yeah, you?"

"Yeah." "I'm gonna make breakfast for us," he said. By this time I was very uncomfortable in the position we were in. I rolled over, facing him, and he looked at me with wide baggy eyes and his hair a mess and his mouth open and he had bad breath. Well, it was morning, I had bad breath too. I had to sit up.

"What," he said.

"My head hurts."

My dick started to shrink in his hand and he went down there and started sucking on it real slow and deep and it cranked back up in his mouth, up his throat. He was doing this very slowly. He was very good at it. It felt very good.

"Al," I said.

"Mmgh?"

"C'mere," I said, tugging slightly at his armpits. He looked up at me with his wet face.

"C'mere," I said again, tapping my chest. He aligned his body along mine and pressed against me. His breath smelled good now and he didn't care about how mine smelled.

In a while we got up and he went to make breakfast. I pissed for the longest time. From the kitchen he said, "You can use my toothbrush—the blue one." Which I did even though I had my own in my gym bag.

I walked around, pretty nosy. There was a room with bunk beds and Yankee and Giant pennants on the wall and dirty clothes all over the place, or maybe they were clean. A Little League baseball uniform, thrown over a chair, said CARBONE'S FUNERAL HOME on the back of it. Another door, his parents' I figured, was shut.

"What are you doing?" hollered Al.

"Nothing," I said.

In the kitchen there were cartons of milk and o.j. and a loaf of white bread on a round yellow formica table. There was a note stuck on to the refrigerator door with one of those rubbery magnet things—Batman—that said, "Alfred, Do not use right front burner."

"How do you like your eggs?" Al said, bareassed, globbing margarine into a frying pan.

"You making bacon?"

"Uh huh."

"Over hard and mixed up with the bacon."

It was nice and everything, him making breakfast, but I didn't know what to do. I wanted us still to be touching. It was weird to suddenly be acting all regular.

His ass jiggled as he scrambled the eggs in the pan and when he shifted his weight to reach for something. I got up and went over there and held on to his waist. He turned and smiled and gave me a semi-sloppy kiss. I sat down again and closed the milk and o.j. cartons. I got up and went over by the counter. "Where are the forks and stuff?"

"In there." He pointed with his chin.

I put them on the table. There were yellow paper napkins in a white plastic netlike napkin holder with a red apple on each side. I sat down again. Whenever Al shifted his weight his toes would lift at the middle knuckle and the thin narrow bones would stick out all the way up his arch. I looked down at the table, which had crumbs on it and crusty ketchup stains and some other stains that I didn't know what they were.

"Something the matter?" he asked.

"No," I said, not knowing what it was that was the matter.

This crummy feeling kept increasing the more I fought it. While we ate I began to feel odd being naked.

"Nice day out," he said.

"Yeah." I wondered what we—I—would do all day. I chewed each piece of eggs, bacon and toast looking at my plate or his hands. I couldn't look at him for some reason. Then he got up and came over to me and put his hand under my arm and whispered, "C'mere, Billy." He got one of his brother's robes from their room and we went in his room and he gave me his robe to put on and he put his brother's on. My robe smelled like him and his smelled like chocolate milk. He flopped down on the bed, grinning.

I sprawled on top of him and picked at the few little hairs on his chest and he brushed my hair back with his fingers and we grinned, looking into each other.

"Okay?" He wrapped his legs around me.

"I felt weird—"

"Does this feel okay?"

"Yeah."

"—Billy."

"Alfred."

He poked me in the side.

"I saw that note on the refrigerator."

"My mother calls me that," he laughed.

"Al-fred!" I imitated a mother calling a kid. We rolled over, me on my back, him on top, and we looked from one eye to the other. "I can see my face," I said.

"Me too."

"All distorted. My nose is huge. Yours must be enormous." He jabbed me in the side again. Then we kissed, a million times, just on the lips.

"—Billy—"

"I'm gonna call you Alfred."

"No, you're not."

"—Alfred—"

"—Billy—"

"Al?"

"Yeah?"

"I really like you."

"Yeah?"

"—Mm hm—"

"How much?"

"A whole lot."

"—You do?—"

"—Yeah—" He put his head down on my chest and I smelled his mussed-up hair.

"You smell good."

"So do you."

"You taste good."

"You taste great."

A dog started to bark. "Oh shit," he said. "I forgot to feed the dog."

"Your grandparents' dog?"

"Yeah." He sprang up onto his knees and got up. "I'll be right back."

I wandered around. In the living room were our clothes thrown here and there, and my gym bag. Also the empty wine glasses. I looked out the kitchen window. Down below was a small backyard surrounded by a chain link fence, surrounded by other small backyards. There was a fig tree in the far right corner. Green and orange tomatoes were growing in rows between the house and the tree, along one side of an upside-down U-shaped brick walk that went by the tomatoes and turned left at the fig tree. There was no grass. The rest was flowers. Big ones, nothing but very tall ones, like sunflowers along the left-hand fence, and shorter ones, about two–three feet tall all over the place, all different colors. I don't know what they're called. And bees buzzing around. A green curled-up hose and a big plastic watering can, and a beach chair with yellow webbing, open on the brick walk on the left. I thought that was all, but then I noticed, right in the middle and almost submerged, a statue of that saint who's a monk that always has a bird on one shoulder and on one finger. I liked this backyard very much. I wanted to be outside. I went and took a hot shower. It felt good. In the middle of it Al came in there with me and we soaped each other up and washed each other's hair real vigorously but it was all becoming—I don't know—I wanted to be alone for some reason.

We got dressed. Al said, "What do you feel like doing?"

"Well, I guess I better go home." He looked disappointed. "I have a lot of things to do," I said. "I have finals this week and everything."

"Yeah, so do I."

"I haven't studied much."

"Me neither."

I picked up my gym bag. "You're gonna drive me home, right?"

He stepped toward me and, running his hands up and down my arms, said, "Why don't we take a ride out to Jones Beach or someplace?"

"Well, I've really got to study. I'd like to do that—go to the beach with you, though. Can we go when school is over?"

He smiled. "Yeah." He put his arms around me and squeezed and I did the same, looking at the door. "That'll be great," he said. "Yeah."

"Is that your mom?"

She was kneeling on a plastic cushion, planting marigold plugs in the border along the driveway. "Uh huh," I said, gripping the car door handle. She stopped and looked up. I opened the door.

"I'll call you later," he said, and squeezed my thigh.

"Okay, bye." I got out and shut the door without looking back and went for the house. When I got to the stoop I realized the car hadn't moved. I turned. My mother was watching us through sunglasses and Al looked at me with a real serious puss on his face— imitating me. He saluted stiffly and then flashed a grin and pulled out and drove off. As I ran up the stoop my mother said, "Billy honey—" and I heard my father mowing on the side of the house.

Inside, I was still feeling Al from head to toe and my chest was thumping, skipping beats. The mowing sound came in through the front door and in the back, through the kitchen window. The curtain fluttered once. I felt the blood rushing through me. I went into my room and looked around at everything, my eyes adjusting to the inside light. The alarm clock had stopped. My plastic models of dogs and wild animals stood there looking at me or at each other or at opposite walls like nothing had happened. I put my gym bag on the bed, forgetting to empty all the wet stuff that was still in it from the meet the night before. I smelled different, of strange kinds of soap and shampoo and toothpaste. My clothes were all crumpled and grungy and matted and I thought of changing but I didn't because if I moved an arm or turned my head I would suddenly get a whiff of Al—or of me and Al—and I'd try to repeat the movement and sometimes it would work and sometimes it wouldn't. McCarthy on the poster looked dumb, like the photographer had physically positioned his head like that with his hands, the way a barber shoves your head around. From outside I heard my parents arguing: something about the marigolds. Then another whiff of Al. I got sad and wondered why the hell I wanted to leave and be alone. I figured he'd still be driving home. To study for finals, like me. I ran back out with a bunch of books and sat on the stoop in the sun. "Hi."

"Hi, honey," my mother said with a genial type of voice while she pulled marigold plugs—every other one—out of the ground like she was annoyed at them. She had planted marigold *seeds* in April but they didn't grow because she planted them in fistfuls according to my father.

"Was that the boy you stayed over with, Billy?" she asked, still tearing out those marigolds.

"Yeah. Why are you pulling them out?"

"Your *father* says I planted them too close together."

"You *did* plant them too close together." This was my father. "They multiply." He was crouched over the jammed relic of a lawnmower.

"He drives a car?" my mother asked me, ignoring him.

I opened my ancient history textbook at random. "Yeah."

"Isn't that the same boy who picks you up to go campaigning?"

"Uh huh."

"What's his name—Al?"

I was thumbing through artists' conceptions of what ruined temples and palaces once looked like.

"Billy, what's his name? Al?"

"Mm hm."

"How did it go?—did you . . . what happened to your lip?"

"Nothing."

She put her sunglasses on top of her head. "Did you win the swimming race?"

"Yeah." Little people in togas were pointing and gesturing. I had penciled a balloon in above one guy's head: "Hey! Plato! You seen Socrates around here anywhere?" His friend was pointing to the top of some temple, saying, "Ain't that him way up there?" And there was Socrates, drawn by me, balancing by one foot on this tower with an exclamation point and two beads of sweat coming out of his head.

"Billy. Billy, I'm talking to you."

"I'm trying to study."

"I thought you were staying over with a boy from school, from your team."

"He was coming to the meet to see his cousin—"

"Who was? This Al?"

"Yeah." It would have felt weird to say his name to them. "His cousin's on the Mount team."

"That damn weed killer don't kill nothin'," my father muttered, unclogging dandelions from the blades of the lawnmower.

Looking at him, my mother said to me, "*What*, honey?"

I looked up at her. "He came to see his cousin who's on the Mount team and we all stayed over."

"I hope you thanked his mother."

I penciled a lawnmower into the hands of a guy who was gaping around in the Hanging Gardens of Babylon. I pictured Al on the beach chair in his backyard among all those tall flowers and tomatoes and the fig tree with huge pre-law books on his lap and on the brick walk next to him.

"I *said*, did you eat anything today?"

"*Yeah we had breakfast.*"

"What did you have?" she asked, lighting a cig.

"Ma, I'm trying to *study. For finals*, okay?"

"Don't be so fresh."

"Well, I don't feel like sitting inside and you keep asking me a million questions." I wondered if Al would hear the phone from outside if it rang.

My mother, finished with the marigolds, was now sweeping dirt off the cement ledge back into the dirt border. My father, the lawnmower unclogged, was wiping his back with a handkerchief.

"You want me to do that?" I asked him.

"Sure—if you want. Or you feel like painting the johnny pump?"

My mother, still sweeping, started shaking her head.

"Okay," I said. I like painting the johnny pump. I do it every year.

She stopped. "He has *tests* to study for. He doesn't have time to do that."

"Oh, *al*right, excuse *me*. Wrong again. As usual," and he resumed mowing.

I ran inside and got my transistor radio and ran back out. Grabbing my books, I said, "See ya later," and tore off down the block toward the water.

"*Where are you going?*" my mother hollered after me.

"*Down by the wall!*" I yelled back.

"*Daddy's gonna pick up Italian heroes later! WHAT KIND DO YOU WANT—VEAL PARMIGIAN?!*"

"YEAH!" I hollered. Al parmigian, I thought, laughing out loud. I sprinted down and over to the wall and stood facing the water on one of the rocks. I tore off my shirt and inhaled it like it was a rose or new shoes or a Christmas tree or a fresh Brillo pad— only better than all those combined. I laid down on my favorite slab of rock and, resting an ankle on an upraised knee, tapped one foot on the rock to the music and the other one in the air, staring at the sky, grinning like an idiot.

WHEN I GOT HOME I CHANGED MY clothes because my underwear was itchy but I didn't take a shower. The things in my room no longer looked totally dumb, just sort of dumb. I wound the alarm clock. I studied for short periods of time. Every now and then I didn't think about Al, forgot that he said he'd call me. During one of those moments the phone rang and it was him. I pictured him not in the house I had been in but in the one I had imagined when I talked to him on the phone those other times before I had ever been there. The conversation was lots of sweet nothings in my ear and in his which I liked quite a lot even though it was pretty corny and I don't feel like going into it in total detail.

That following week we both had finals so we talked on the phone every night. But we really wanted to see each other so we did. We worked in the office on a mailing, stuffing envelopes with Brendan.

With only two weeks to go till the primary and two months till the Democratic convention in Chicago, practically everything was pretty fouled up. Nationally, the Kennedy people didn't like McCarthy. They thought he should have dropped out of the race when Kennedy entered it, so they were either moving to Humphrey, because of his civil rights record supposedly, or to someone named McGovern, a friend of the Kennedys.

Harold got a haircut and was smoking two-three cigarettes at once with Band-Aids on his fingernails. Several volunteers wanted to put a picture of Kennedy in the window with black around it but Harold wouldn't allow it and it caused a big argument. They said he was crass and unfeeling and that's what I thought at the time too, but he was just doing his job. A left-wing dove peace candidate was on thin ice in that district as it was, never mind putting a picture of Robert Kennedy in the window with black bunting around it. After campaigning all over New England and the Midwest, Harold said that ours was one of the most redneck hawk districts he had been in.

When we were done in the office, Al and I went up to Nathan's on the Sprain. I was wondering if he had seen that man about that job yet but I didn't mention it and neither did he.

On the way back in the car I asked him if his parents were going away that weekend. He shook his head no.

There was nowhere to go to be together. Then I got a brainstorm. "You know my aunt on the Shore?"

"Yeah."

"Maybe we could go down there—like for the weekend."

"Oh yeah?" he said, kind of uneasy.

"Yeah, she lives there alone and it's this big house with all these rooms."

"But won't she be around?"

"Well yeah, she'll be around, she'll probably be around sometimes but she'll also be showing houses. She's a real-estate agent, I mean she owns her own real-estate company." He started unwrapping a piece of gum. "And anyway, she's very cool. She doesn't act like an aunt."

"But at night—she'll figure out what's going on, if I'm sleeping in the same room as you." He stuck the gum in his mouth. "You know."

"I don't think so." I was kind of annoyed that I had to convince him. I didn't think my aunt would care even if she knew Al and I were fucking our brains out right under her roof, but I didn't say that to Al. I think she knew I liked guys, and not only that, she thought it was fine. Like remember the time she said Evan and Kevin sounded cute and I said Oh they *are* and she winked? That's why I thought it would be totally cool to go down there with Al and not have to be all secret about everything and pretend we were just pals, which we *were*, we were pals, but not *just* pals.

So I said, "She'll probably be gone during the day—Saturday at least. But maybe not, I mean I can't guaran*tee* it. And anyway, boys always sleep in the same room when they sleep over."

"Okay," he laughed. "It sounds good." He looked at me, chewing with a big grin. "Sounds great."

I called her that night and she said, "Sure, come down and bring your friend." I was quite excited about it.

At school that week, at finals, some guys on my team sort of didn't look at me, or looked away when I looked at them. I wondered if it was because I lost that event at the invitational or because they thought I was a homosexual. I figured it was because I lost the event.

After my last final on Thursday I went down to the pool locker area with Evan and Kevin to clean out our lockers. I was walking between them. I was hoping Mr. Bieniwicz wouldn't be around and he wasn't.

Two seniors from the team were coming toward us. One of them said, "Ooh, look! It's Eek and Ike the Spacemen!" I thought that was pretty funny. I had never heard that one before.

As they passed us, the other one with his hand cupped to his mouth said, "And their trusty companion, Bruce the—" Bruce the something or other. I didn't hear the last word. I stopped. Bruce was a faggot name.

Evan and Kevin moved in to me from both sides and propelled me along. I just sort of obeyed them and didn't resist. The two seniors kept going the other way, laughing.

Most people who call themselves pacifists are really just weak-assed wimps if you ask me. Faggots, most people would say. Evan and Kevin were never scared, though. And as I know I already told you, they did not care what anyone thought of them or said to them, anyway.

We didn't say anything about it. I went to my locker and they went to theirs which was two alcoves away and I heard them whispering. I sat on the bench. I couldn't understand what they were saying.

Outside, they asked me if I wanted to go to a Kinks concert at the Fillmore downtown on Saturday. They said they had an extra ticket.

I looked from Evan to Kevin. Their hair was blowing straight up. I had never done anything like that with them. In fact, the thought never even occurred to me.

Instead of saying yes or no, I said, "How come you have an extra ticket?"

"Because someone else was going and now he can't come," Kevin said.

I wondered who this "he" was who sounded so mysterious to me. I said that I'd really like to go, but that I had something else to do.

They asked me what.

I told them about going to the Shore. I told them about the lifeguard job.

They kept twitching their overbites.

I told them I was going down there with my friend who was at the swim meet.

"Well, have a great time," said Kevin. "Yeah," said Evan.

"Thanks," I said. "You too."

We stood there. They were grinning. I kept looking from one to the other. I said, "Maybe we could go to some other concert in a couple of weeks or sometime."

"Okay." "Yeah."

"Maybe you two could come down to the Shore, like for a weekend this summer."

"Definitely." They gave me their number and I gave them mine.

CHAPTER

19

WHEN AL PICKED ME UP FRIDAY HE was wearing cut-offs and sneakers with no socks and so was I which was a sheer coincidence and it felt very romantic to be going on this weekend trip with him. On the George Washington Bridge he told me that he got that job with the Regular Democratic Club. He didn't seem too hepped up about it, though. In fact, he was sort of brushing it off, or maybe he was just pretending to be brushing it off.

"Yeah, so I'll be working with this guy who's the district leader," he said. "And listen to this—I may be going to Chicago as an alternate delegate. Some old geezer's dying, so they're gonna need a replacement."

"You mean your name would be on the ballot and everything?"

"Yeah."

"So you'd have to win first."

He looked at me funny and lifted four fingers of his right hand off the steering wheel. "Yeah."

I wasn't mad, but I got that thumb-pressed-on-the-chest feeling. "What makes you think they'll pick you?"

He said they needed an Italian name—and someone willing to pay their way to Chicago. They'd pay for the hotel but not the plane. "I figure it's worth it for the experience," he said. "—You know. And it's practically definite—this old guy'll be dead any second, from what they tell me."

"I'll be campaigning against you in other words."

He sort of laughed. "Yeah, but even if I'm elected, alternate delegates hardly ever get to vote at these things."

When we passed Jersey City, he pointed with his chin over to the left. "That's where my sister lives, and her husband." He said the word "husband" with a smirk, like he thought he was a jerk. "Great place, Jersey City—fuckin' slum." We didn't say much for a while.

Then, in that whispery voice like on the phone, he said, "Billy—"

"Yeah?"

"I don't want any bad feelings between you and me."

"Me neither."

"Because I really like you." He looked at my knee for a couple of seconds, and then back on the road. He took my hand and squeezed it hard, almost hurting it.

When we got to my aunt's house it was dark and you could hear the shore against the beach in a low-tide pebbly manner. It's a white wooden house with an unpainted deck that faces the ocean. Wooden steps run down to the beach and there's a flagpole on the deck with a flag that never gets taken in.

One of the dogs, a Wheaton terrier, came charging out from around the side and jumped up and down all over us and licked us and smelled us like crazy. My aunt came out with a bottle of beer and shook our hands and said that she was glad to see us fellas. She showed us to a room on the first floor with a double bed.

"This is the only clean bedroom," she said. "I hope you boys don't mind sharing a bed."

We said Oh no, it was okay.

The three of us sat on the deck that looked out to the ocean and drank bottles of beer in the salt breeze and watched the three dogs run around on the beach below where the tide was coming in. Besides the Wheaton, she has a golden retriever and a little mutt—part beagle, part dachshund and part something else. Occasionally one of them would run all the way up the stairs and sniff around us and look at us from one to the other and then look out at the other two and tear ass back down the steps to the beach. My aunt would laugh when they did this and watch them and take the rubber band out of her ponytail and then put it back in. She was wearing those stretch kind of pants with loops that go under your feet, flip-flops and a sweatshirt that said MCCC on it. I asked her what it stood for. "Monmouth County Community College," she said. "I teach an adult ed course there in real estate," which is something I didn't know about her.

We were sitting on beach chairs. Al was on the edge of his, leaning forward, holding his beer in both hands. Whenever he noticed that I was looking at him, he'd smile with his eyes into me. On the side of the house was a tall locust tree in bloom and whenever there was a breeze, which was quite often, small white petals would waft over us onto the deck and down to the beach. We barbecued hamburgers and ate them and potato salad on paper plates at this redwood table and drank more beer.

My aunt asked how my mother and father were and I said Fine. We got pretty high and we were telling her about the whole McCarthy thing and Al gave her his I'm-going-to-be-the-first-Italian-president-of-the-United-States spiel, which really sounded kind of dumb to me. She said, "Ohh, mm hm." I wondered how many people he told that to.

He asked her if it was okay to smoke a joint and she said yes but she didn't want any. The joint made me a little paranoid and I wanted to be alone with Al. After a while we cleaned up and we locked the dogs in this pen or cage-type thing under the house on the beach and then we all went to bed. Her room was on the second floor. When we shut our door we both instantly took our clothes off and collided into each other and fell on the bed and it was even better than the last time and very extreme and kind of unbearable in a great sort of way. Any crummy feelings that were building up about Al disappeared.

In the middle of the night I woke up and he wasn't there. I

turned on the light and for some reason the first thing I did was to see if his bag and stuff were gone. It was all still there. I went out on the deck without putting any clothes on. It was high tide. He was sitting on the bottom step down by the beach. I went down there. It was very dark, with no moon. He was naked, wet and salty.

"Hi," I said, sitting down next to him.

He put his arm around me and looked at me. His brows were all knitted up like when you're concerned about something, or thinking a lot. His lips were kind of in a pout. He pulled me towards him.

"What's the matter," I said.

"Billy, I'm really crazy about you."

I put my foot on top of his. "Al—"

"Yeah?"

I was looking at his shoulder. "I really think I love you."

He moved his hand to the back of my neck and massaged it real strongly, pressing with his thumb. "I know I love you," he said.

"I think about you all the time when I'm not with you," I said.

"I think about you all the time too."

"You know . . ."

"—What."

"When I woke up just now I thought you left in the car."

"I can't believe you thought that." He seemed really hurt.

I took him and pulled him down so he was face-up in my lap. I held his head and felt his wet curls. He looked up at me and parted his lips and opened his mouth and his eyes closed. I went into him and licked all the salt off his mouth. I lifted my head.

"I don't think I did so great on my finals," he said. "I couldn't study."

"Me neither."

"I know you think I'm a shithead for working for Humphrey and everything—"

"Well—"

"Those people will be a good place to start if I really want to go into politics."

"It's okay."

"The primary will be over soon, and even if McCarthy wins some delegates in New York he can't win the convention." He sounded like he was quoting someone again. I looked out at the ocean, holding his head. "And Humphrey's gotta be better than Nixon," he said.

"I'm not so sure about that."

"But, see, the thing is . . ." He plopped himself on the sand and stuck his feet on my lap and I massaged them and his toes.

"What," I said.

The dogs started whining under the house.

"What I mean is in the long run . . ."

"What about it."

"That feels great . . . I mean, you can't be a politician and be— you know—what we're doing." I stopped rubbing his foot. He went on. "I mean, you've got to be married and everything and have kids and everything."

"So don't be a politician."

"My mother and father still think I'm a 'late bloomer,'" he said. "But they're not gonna keep believing that for long. They expect me to get married and have kids and all that—you know, irregardless of the politician thing."

I remembered when he made a big deal in the Gold Star about saying he didn't have a girlfriend and now here he was talking about a wife. "Why don't you do what you want," I said, "not what they want?"

He glanced a look at me for a second, then fixed on some point a few feet away on the sand. My idea was not something that had never occurred to him, I don't think. He had thought about it a lot but figured it was too costly. It was out of the question. I dropped his foot and stood up. Al really was a politician and I wasn't. I mean, even if he never actually went into politics, he was still a politician, if you see what I mean.

I stood there, rigid, watching him. He left his foot where I had dropped it and continued to stare at the sand next to him, like he was looking at, but not examining, one particular grain. The locust tree kind of moaned toward us, and white petals plummeted down in a heap.

"What," I heard him say, very still.

"What about you and me," I said.

He started dumping handfuls of sand and locust petals on his ankles, covering them. I felt angry in some new kind of way. I was glad but I hated it. "You're full of shit," I said, and walked toward the water.

He overtook me and blocked me, stood facing me. It was like the time under the tree after the meet, only different. Something was closing, getting shut off.

"You've got no fucking balls, Al."

He jabbed me on the chest, once. *"Don't give me that shit again, Billy."*

"Quit *jab*bin' me," I said, shoving him back with both hands.

We stood there for what seemed a very long time, just blazing at each other, but it was probably only a second. With the heels of his hands he knocked me down on my back on the sand and jumped on me, straddling me, hauling his arm back—a fist, his mouth in a slit.

My aunt's voice floated over from the deck: "Are you boys out there?"

Al's whole body racked solid. "Don't say anything," he whispered, his fist still raised.

The dogs were going crazy now.

My aunt: "Billy, is that you?" She didn't put the outside light on.

"Don't move." He was frozen stiff. For the first time with Al I wanted to press the ejector button.

"We should answer her," I said.

"Don't."

I didn't hear her coming down the steps but all of a sudden the gate of the dog pen was opening and the dogs were yelping and jumping all over us, licking us and everything.

My aunt was going back up the stairs in a robe. "Just let them out if you come out here at night, okay?"

"Oh, okay!" I hollered. "Sorry!"

"It's okay!" and she went inside. She must have thought we were total jerks.

The dogs ran away, down by the shoreline. Al's head slowly bowed and he laid it on my chest and slipped his hands under my back in slow motion and held on to my lats and shuddered, still straddling me, his knees tight around my ribcage. I put my hands on his head, in his hair, and turned and looked out at the dogs. We were very gritty.

After a while he said, "I'm just a jerk, Billy, I don't deserve you. I'm just a big jerk. I'm a coward."

I didn't say anything. I agreed with him. But I had told him I loved him and I meant it and he had told me he loved me and I think he meant it.

I was massaging his back. He looked up at me. His eyes were all puffy. After a few seconds he said, "I wish we were on Mars." He stretched his legs out straight and laid down on top of me and rested his head again on my chest. But I couldn't help twisting a knife. "Why don't you go to a shrink and get cured?" I said.

Looking out at the ocean, he lifted his head an inch off my chest.

"—If you hate it so much."

"Hate what."

"Being a homosexual."

"I can't stand that word," he said, rolling off me onto his side and supporting his head with his hand. He started tossing sand on my stomach. "I'm crazy about you. How could you say I hate it?" I didn't say anything. He quit throwing sand at me. Then he laid down flat on his back.

The Wheaton ran over and stood with his two front paws on Al's chest, looking at me, his tongue hanging out his mouth, panting. He looked like he was laughing.

I put my hands behind my head.

Al just looked up at the dog standing on him. Then he said, "Billy—"

I looked at the dog. I didn't say What? and Al didn't say whatever he was going to say. He lifted the dog off him.

I stood up and walked into the surf. Al caught up to me and we dove in and swam around but it was very cold and no fun. We put the dogs away and rinsed off under the outdoor shower. We went to bed and fell immediately to sleep. Well, I fell asleep.

"What the fuck are you doing?" I said, bolting awake.

Our hair was still wet and our crotches damp in the dark in the bed and something was trying to wriggle itself up my ass—Al's pinky.

"Ssh," he whispered. "How does it feel?"

"Like I don't want it there. Get it out."

"Wait a minute." He hopped up and got a tube of this greasy stuff called K-Y out of his bag. "I'm not going to do anything you won't like. I promise."

I was on my back. He lifted my legs and spread some of the goo on his middle finger and wormed it in very slowly to the first knuckle. "You feel that?"

"Of course I feel it."

"Relax that muscle."

"I can't."

"Just relax it. You're not used to relaxing it, but you can. Just relax it."

I tried to relax but it kept tightening. His finger was lapping around in there. I kind of groaned, I think. For a while I didn't tighten, but then I did, around his finger. "Yeeow!"

"Relax it, baby."

Something was starting to feel sort of good. Al looked up at me, grinning. "That's it, that's it, Billy." He was massaging something that felt good. "It's very sensitive," he said, "you feel that?" I exhaled through my mouth. "It's the prostate," he said. "I can feel it throb against my finger."

I was beginning to loosen up for longer periods of time. I was hard as a rock and so was he. He said, "I could make you come just by massaging that."

"Go ahead," I said.

"You want me to fuck you, baby?"

"—I don't know."

"I'll stop whenever you want me to."

"—Okay."

"You sure?"

"Yeah."

With his finger still up there, he started to grease up his cock.

"Let me do it," I said. He handed me the tube and I slicked him up. It bucked and kicked in my hand and he went, "Oooh," with his eyes closed. He was rubbing my prostate and every time he did, my cock stood up, then splat against my belly.

He pulled his finger out and pressed in against my asshole. With his two hands like greasy vises, he held my ankles back over my head. My knees were touching my shoulders. He pushed in and I tightened and my cock sprang up. "Ohhh—*oww!*" I yelled, gritting my teeth.

He held the head there. "Relax, relax, relax, relax, Billy, relax." I relaxed. "Push it in," I said.

But he held it like that, pulsing, just the head inside me. He leaned down over me and stuck his tongue down my throat and I sucked on it as he very very slowly glided his cock in. I found that I could keep loose by concentrating, then after a while I didn't even have to think about it. He sat up slowly, a long line of spit connecting his lower lip to my tongue.

"Look," he said. "Feel it with your hand."

I felt the underbase of his cock, throbbing like mad. I felt his balls which were right up against my ass. He knelt there, us looking into each other, then he flexed it inside me, once. "Wheew," I said, closing my eyes, grinning. He chuckled, put some more grease on his hand and slowly pulled out and as he pushed back in, mine leapt straight up. He grabbed it with his hand.

I was just moaning. I couldn't believe it. It was better than anything. And another thing was the way it looked—Al's body bucking and rippling, humping. I reached up and held on to his lats. He held my feet together and started sucking on my toes! I started slapping his ass as he rammed in and I lifted my ass up off the bed ramming into him, meeting him. Then we fell off the bed, crashing onto the floor. My back was on the floor and my ass in the air and he was over me. I tried not to yell but I was going to explode. He put his hand over my mouth and I sucked on his hypothenar muscle, that fleshy side part, and made sort of like wheezing sounds or squeaking sounds as I shot all over my face and chest.

"Pull it out! *Pull it out!*" I pushed at the top of his thighs and he pulled out and his cock bounced at my face and then it was still and then it pumped and without touching it he shot straight out all over my face and I stuck my tongue out and caught a big glob. He was all wobbly and we were both grinning like when drunk cowboys get socked in the jaw and they lay there with their eyes half open, grinning with birds tweeting around their heads. He was soaked and so was I and he fell down on top of me with a splap and a squish and we rolled all around, licking each other and sucking every part of our bodies till we fell asleep in some crazy position on the floor.

In the morning my ass was real sore—all day in fact—but otherwise I felt great. We finally got up and took a shower together, then we put on our swimsuits. We were going to go check out the beach where I would work. I was combing my hair and Al went into the kitchen.

"*Oh shit,*" I heard him say and I went in there.

"What."

"Look at this." He picked a note up off the table. It said,

Good morning, boys—
   Gone to show some houses. Should be back around 4. Do what you want. There's food. You know where the town beach is.
   I'd like to talk to you later.

Love,
Marge

I knew what he was thinking.

"She heard us," he said, all alarmed, his hands gripping the back of a chair.

I didn't bother saying So what or It doesn't matter or anything like that. Grabbing a couple of donuts I said, "Let's go," and went out to the deck and ran down the steps with Al right behind me. It was sunny and warm, dry, not hazy, a perfect day. We ran out on to the beach and the dogs started barking so we let them out and took them with us, jogging along the shore, through the breakers. I didn't feel one bit odd the way I did the day we woke up in his house after that first time. Last night we really, actually FUCKED. It was more than fucking, though. Well, I guess maybe you know what it was.

Anyway, at the town beach there was hardly anybody around except out in the water were three kids in wet suits sitting on those small-type surfboards, waiting, within earshot of one another, but not talking. Every five minutes or so, one of them would spot a good wave coming, he'd scramble onto his board and surf in unsteadily, wobbly, sometimes not all the way. They seemed sort of new to it but they were very intent and serious about getting the hang of it, getting it right.

Three lifeguard stands were on their sides and dragged up by this retaining wall for the winter. We sat on the wall, leaning forward, our hands holding on to the edge, watching the surfers. We walked around and went swimming and ate hot dogs and stuff but we hardly said anything all day.

My aunt waved from the deck when she saw us coming and I waved back. The dogs dropped in the shade under the house and from the bottom of the steps I asked her if they needed water or anything. Al stopped and stood next to me.

"No, no," she said. "There's a leak in that hose down there, and they drink out of it."

We climbed the stairs. She was working at the table on some papers with a calculator. There was a half-full bottle of beer and one empty one. A towel was wrapped around her head and she had a terry-cloth robe on.

I hopped up on the wooden rail, facing her, flicking sand off my toes. Al sat on a beach chair and crossed a leg, an ankle on a knee, and fiddled with his ear.

My aunt looked up from her work, at me and then at Al and I think she saw how nervous he was. I asked her what she wanted to talk to us about.

"Oh, is that it?" she said, shutting off the calculator. "It seems silly now. It's just that you kept waking me up last night. I don't mean when you were outside. Later—inside." Al blushed and watched his foot. "Al," she said, straddling the bench, "you understand that it's just the *racket* that was a problem."

She started to dry her hair with the towel. "I'd forgotten all about that note," she said, laughing. "I was furious when I wrote it." She's got this sort of contagious laugh. I started to laugh and then Al smiled sort of shy-like. I told her I was sorry about waking her up.

Al leaned forward, looking down, his forearms on his knees. I was still flicking sand off my toes even though there was no more sand on them. He squeezed his hands together and his knuckles turned white. My aunt took a slug of beer, got up and went inside.

"This *is* another planet," he said. I couldn't tell if he was relieved or shocked or what.

I got off the rail and sat on the bench, leaning forward towards him, in the same position he was in. He reached his right foot over and stuck his big toe and the second toe in between the same toes on my left foot and we sort of squished them around.

My aunt made something called paella which was very very good and Al and I cut all the vegetables which is something neither one of us had ever done before but I think we did it alright. All night Al acted real uncomfortable around my aunt like he hadn't been up till then.

When we went to bed, at first we said we better not wake her up, so we were messing around kind of quiet-like but then I wanted to fuck Al and he said No, we would make too much noise. But after a while he wanted to fuck me and I said I thought you said we'd make too much noise? and he said Oh, we can try to be quiet and I said No if I couldn't fuck him, then he couldn't fuck me and I know this all sounds stupid and lame but that's what happened and then we just laid there on the bed, a mile of space in between us.

I don't feel like going into all the details but he wouldn't even tell me the real reason why he didn't want me to do it and it was pretty annoying and it made me mad. I asked him if he was ever fucked before and he said no which was very surprising to me. I said that he must have fucked other guys—or girls—based on how expert he was at it. He said he had *never* fucked a girl but that he used to fuck that guy all the time who when Al and I were in his parents' house the night of the invitational when they went away for the weekend and he told me that he and that boy down the block used to give each other blowjobs—remember that? Well, he said that he used to fuck that guy's ass all the time. But he himself never got fucked and didn't want to. I think he thought that getting fucked up the ass meant GETTING FUCKED UP THE ASS, if you see what I mean. Also, I felt like he was treating me like a girl in a way since only he could do the fucking. So I wouldn't let him, even though I know I would have liked it. "Getting fucked" isn't GETTING FUCKED, it's fucking *both* of you at the same time, if you do it right, if you see what I mean, like the previous night.

He eventually fell asleep laying way over on the other side of the bed on his back. I just laid there and watched him and watched him and in a while I fell asleep away over on my side of the bed. Up until now there weren't any sides of the bed.

I had a dream of Al at a beach coming out of the water dripping wet and taking a black Ace comb out of a bag and standing there, water trickling down his thighs with some honey-brown voluptuous sultry female laying on a blanket leaning on an elbow tossing him a hip taking him in with a sad smile on her face while he's gazing out at the ocean, regarding it, dripping, combing his hair sort of broodily. Then she says, "Darling, I am with child."

When I woke up in the morning he was all wrapped around me like the time at his house. But I wanted to get up. I wanted to go home. I squeezed out from under his leg and arm and got up and went to the bathroom. When I came out he was still in the same position, only with his eyes open, staring at nothing.

I sat on the bottom of the bed and looked at him. I could only see his right eye. It moved in my direction, and then back into space. We just sat there like that. Then, with half his mouth sort of muffled by the pillow, he said, "You wanna go home?"

"Yeah," I said.

"So do I." He sprang up and without looking at me he went into the bathroom and shut the door. We never, neither one of us, ever shut the door when we went to the bathroom. When he came out he started to get dressed. He was turning a T-shirt right side out. "Well," he said, "aren't you gonna put your clothes on?"

I just sat there, looking at this bush of wild roses that grows outside the window.

He started picking at his curls in the mirror. "I think I'll get a haircut this week," he said. "I'm sick of these stupid curls."

I got up and started to get dressed.

"Billy, hurry up."

I snapped my cut-offs. *"Fuck you."*

He was standing there with his arms folded. He picked up his bag and tossed his keys in the air, caught them with a backhand and while walking out of the room said, "Fuckin' nuthouse—fuckin' Mars."

The car started up but it didn't pull out; it just sat there idling. I didn't know if he was trying to decide whether to split by himself or if he was waiting for me.

I spotted a pair of his BVDs stuffed under a radiator. They must have been tossed over there when we were in a big hurry to get our clothes off Friday night after the barbecue on the deck. I listened to the motor running and stared at the underwear from where I stood. I went and picked it up and sat on the bed and put it to my face, covered my face with it, inhaling it. When I looked up, there he was standing there leaning against the doorjamb with his hands in his pockets, smiling, his shoulders jumping up and down, like when you laugh with no sound. I pitched the BVDs at him and they fell at his feet. He said, "Billy, we're hooked, I think."

"Why don't you just go," I said.

"You don't want me to go, do you?"

"Yes, I do."

He sat down next to me on the bed. "I'm—"

"Don't say I'm sorry." I got up. "I'm sick of you sayin' that shit." I walked out on the deck. I thought he was a jerk and an asshole but I was crazy about him anyway. Which seemed really sick to me. We were acting like some dumb-ass couple on TV or something who have arguments all the time and then make up. Man and woman couples. It's got to be able to be different with guys. Better. I'm sure of it.

The car was still running. Finally my aunt came out and asked me what was going on.

"I don't know," I said.

"You had a fight?"

"I guess so." I didn't want to face her and she was standing in the door so I went around the side and out front and there's Al just sitting in the car.

"What are you doing?" I said.

"Waiting for you—wasting gas."

I thought of what the ride home would be like—lumpy awkward silence. "I'm gonna take the bus home," I said.

He was mad. He started backing out the driveway.

Once when I was a kid I was supposed to be going somewhere with my parents for the day—maybe here, I can't remember—someplace I liked to go, but I was real mad at them for some reason and I wouldn't go. All I wanted them to do was insist that I go—although I didn't realize that at the time—and force me into the car which they had done *many* times before but not this time. They left and I watched them through the living-room window and ran outside yelling *"Wait! Wait!"* just as the car pulled away. After crying for a couple of hours in the bathtub with no water in it, I played with my Disneykins and had them murder each other by pushing each other off tall buildings—end tables.

As Al was backing out, that whole scene flashed and popped into my head. I ran down the driveway. "Al! Wait up!"

He slammed on the brake and stuck his head and elbow out the window.

I ran up to him. He reached his arm out and grabbed the back of my neck and pulled me down to him mouth to mouth.

I said goodbye to my aunt and I thanked her a lot and apologized a lot for us acting like jerks and everything and she said it was okay, she understood, and I said I'd see her soon and Al and I split.

In the car it wasn't awkward silence but it was lousy anyway. We were straining to be all normal and nice, real careful not to talk about fucking or politics or Al's future career. But we both knew that those things were on both of our minds. When he dropped me off neither one of us said anything about calling the other one.

THE FOLLOWING WEEKEND ON THE last Saturday before the primary I worked all day at this big Mc-Carthy rally—well, a McCarthy rally—at Pelham Bay station. I had a lousy time doing it without Al there. Up until then I had only worked with him, so I hardly even knew anyone else.

His name wasn't actually on the ballot because the old man kicked off too late to change it. So the dead guy won, which meant that Al won. McCarthy won three out of six delegates, probably because *his* name wasn't on the ballot. He also won about half the delegates statewide, the other half divided between Uncommitted and Kennedy, who was also dead. The Peace candidate for senator, O'Dwyer, won the primary, which was an upset, and a lot of the local McCarthy workers were going to work for him now. There was a victory party at a hotel downtown, but I didn't feel like going.

Next day Harold was exhausted and pleased and left with his troop in the bus, bound eventually for Chicago. Brendan was crying because they were all leaving and I told him there were other campaign offices where he could volunteer and we went for an egg cream. I tried to explain to him where the Regular Democratic Club was, but he didn't know what I was talking about or else he was no longer interested.

Anyway, I didn't call Al and he didn't call me and there were only a few days left before I had to go back down to Jersey. I hung around the phone a lot and stared at it and jumped when it rang but it was never him and it was never even for me. Tommy and

Lorraine were gone and Joey wasn't calling for some reason, maybe because I never called him anymore. I didn't want to be around him because I'd have to pretend and lie about everything, like I did around my parents. By lie I mean not mention Al at all. It's not really a lie because you're not saying anything about it, but it's a lie because ordinarily you would say whatever you want—like if this had all happened with a girl.

One night I was just laying on the couch watching TV with pillows stuffed between my legs and my father was watching TV and each half hour or hour he'd change the channel and I'd just watch whatever he put on. It was over a week since the Shore with Al.

My mother came in with an ashtray and said, "Move your feet." She sat on the other end of the couch and lit a cigarette. "What's the matter with you?"

"Nothing's the matter with me."

"What are you moping around all the time for—doing nothing."

"I'm watching TV."

"Since when do you watch TV all night long?"

My father said, "I'm tryna watch this. Go talk inside if you want to talk."

"Aren't there any more dances?" she asked, ignoring him. "Why hasn't Joey called lately?"

My father said, "This is the television room, not a talking room."

"It's a *living* room. I can talk to my son in my own living room without asking your permission, almighty one." She dragged on her cig.

"Well, go talk to *your son* in some other room."

I got up and went into my room and locked the door. I took down the McCarthy poster but not the muscular chart. I laid on my bed and stared at it with its hands outstretched and I outstretched my hands, imagining I was it.

I wanted to call Evan and Kevin but I didn't. I kept hoping they
would call me but they didn't. Not until—well, that comes later.

The phone rang. I ran to answer it.

"Hello?"

"Hi."

"Hi—uh, wait a minute." I brought the phone in my room, my
chest pounding. I sat on the floor, as far from the door as I could
get. "Hi."

"How ya doin'?" A lot of noise on his end.

"What are you, at work?"

Al: "Yeah. What're you doin'?"

"Nothin'. What are you doin'?"

"Nothin'. I'm done here." Then he whispered, "Can you hear
me when I talk this low?"

"Yeah."

"I miss you, baby."

"Don't call me baby."

"Don't you miss me?"

"Yeah." I was picking at my toes. "But you're a jerk."

"Billy . . ."

"What."

"Don't start that—okay?"

I was examining my model of a tiger. The paint job I gave it was
very good.

Al: "You wanna go for pizza?"

"Okay."

"I'll be right over."

"Bye."

Click. That's the way it was. That's the way you decide these
things. You don't decide. You just instantly say okay or no, and I
said okay.

At the Gold Star we were both kind of nervous. We didn't say
anything about why we hadn't called each other all week. He told

me about his job. It had to do with local candidates who had a primary in September. He didn't mention a thing about being an elected Uncommitted alias Humphrey alternate delegate or about his upcoming trip to the Chicago convention. I did an imitation of Harold wiping his glasses and squinting and complaining about The Shits Downtown who wouldn't schedule The Candidate into The District and Al thought it was pretty funny.

Then he leaned forward. He rubbed the table with a thumb. "So, uh, Billy—can I come down to the Shore and visit you when you're down there?"

"I thought you said it was a nuthouse."

"I was mad. I didn't really mean that. It's a great escape place."

Who waltzes in at that very second but Sue and the jerk from the Kathy's swim team, holding hands, and he pulls her over to us although she looked like she didn't really want to and he's smirking and Sue is looking embarrassed while I'm chewing, looking at her, and she's looking at the table or the floor.

Her boyfriend says to me, "Who's this?" thumbing at Al. "Your boyfriend?" And he giggles in that high-pitched manner.

"Jimmy, come *on*," she says to him, and heat ran up my back into my head and ears.

"That's right," I said. "This is my boyfriend." Al was practically under the table. I never thought someone that tan could turn that red but he did, wide-eyed, staring at me.

"Come on, Jimmy," Sue says again, pulling him away while he's giggling, saying, "Okay, let's leave the two homo lover boys alone so they can—" and blah blah blah while I'm looking at Al with my jaw flexed the way Tommy used to clench his.

Al says, "Are you *crazy?* What the fuck did you say that for?! This isn't your aunt's house."

That was it. I split, without looking back, thinking he'd follow me but he didn't. As I walked home from the Gold Star, things that were circling and colliding inside my head about Al formed a solid blob. At my aunt's house when he said, "This *is* another planet," he was shocked, yeah, but not with relief that she was so cool. He was offended that a responsible adult person would think that what we were doing was normal and totally okay with her. He thinks people should put it down, or at least pretend they don't see it.

On that walk home, I hated him for being such a chickenshit. But if you want to know the truth, I hated him even more for not following me. Now I'm glad he didn't. I guess. I don't hate him now. But I think I hate the whole world—except certain people in it.

CHAPTER

21

EVAN AND KEVIN AND AL WERE down here at the Shore for a weekend. It was pouring raining and thundering and the four of us swam out to this big rock that's out in the water. We were just standing on it in our swimsuits as gray black clouds swirled with a rumble and roared, crashing right overhead and parted partially. The sky right above us became grayish gold and the rain was still pouring, quite hard, harder than before.

We heard a motorboat approach from the gloom. You couldn't see the shore now and waves were breaking over the rock, covering it at times up to our knees but with no effect on us. The motorboat was getting closer and there were four people in it, chanting something. Then I saw Tommy in the front of the boat aiming his father's .45-caliber gun at us. I couldn't understand what they were chanting and I don't know who the other three people were, but they were adults. The four of us stood with our arms around each other's shoulders—Evan Kevin Me Al—and then Evan and Kevin twitched their overbites and antennas rose out of their heads—one each—with little green lights on the tips that would glow and dim, glow, and dim.

Tommy was very startled and stopped chanting but the three grown-ups shouted at him, pointing to us with red faces all knitted up and then Tommy resumed chanting and fired off four shots at us but the bullets swirled around our heads and whizzed around and shot right back at them in the boat and hit each one dead, right between the eyes.

That wasn't another lie. I haven't told you any lies ever since I said I wasn't going to. That was a sort of dream I had when I was laying in the sun one day, half awake, next to Kevin who really is here. Evan isn't, but Kevin is. Evan is dead. There is a rock in the water, though.

I'm down on the Shore right now in other words, in the middle of August, sitting on the bottom of the splintery gray-beaten wooden steps that reach up in a zigzag from the beach to my aunt's house. The dogs keep running and jumping all over the place, like on me for example. I've been working six days a week. I'm off today. I like the job quite a lot. I actually saved someone— an old man who got a cramp—and he's been bringing bags of fruit for me and the two other lifeguards ever since. Mainly peaches and apples but also some kinds I've never had before like mangos and something else I can't remember the name of. The two other guards are guys my age and they might have been two of those surfers we saw that day because they have surfboards and wet suits and they're showing me how to surf which I like quite a lot. I don't really hang around with them or anything other than guarding and surfing and they think I'm kind of closed-mouthed probably. Kevin is here, although Evan isn't. Evan is dead. Kevin is the one with the chipped tooth. Sometimes I help little kids build sandcastles and things even though I'm really not supposed to do that while I'm working. I get to sit on one of those white wooden lifeguard stands and look cool in these orange boxer trunks with SEA BRIGHT

27 in white on one hip and a whistle around my neck and everything. Gorgeous girls are constantly flirting with me and so do
some cute guys but I hardly talk to any of them. I'm not rude or
anything, I mean I *talk* to them but I don't flirt back.

My mother calls once a week. We don't say much. I tell her a
few lifeguard stories and then she talks to my aunt. I think they
talk about me. I also talk to Emo on the phone, a lot more often
than I've ever seen her in person. I told her all about Al and I
wasn't at all nervous or anything about how she would react and I
was right because she thought the whole thing was *very sexy*.
That's exactly what she said and she wanted to know all the details.
Now she calls me Hotstuff.

Whenever I think of Al, which is quite often, my insides get hot
from my chest out and down through me like fire, and I exhale
heat. He's in Chicago now. The convention starts this week and
there's all this talk about violence and everything. He just called
me. I had not spoken to him at all since that last time in the Gold
Star. He said he's not going to wear his HHH button anywhere but
in the convention hall. He said when it's over he wants to come
down here and see me. But I told him no. Kevin is here. Evan is
dead. Evan got murdered, knifed in the subway one night and
Kevin got stabbed while trying to help him. He's staying here with
me. Kevin is. His arm is in a sling. He doesn't do too much other
than sit under an umbrella on a chaise lounge on the beach gazing
out at the ocean, regarding it, examining it, with a silent stream of
tears rolling continuously down his face. Which is what he's doing
at the present moment. I never know what to say to him. I sit on
the sand next to him and hold his hand a lot and he grips it tight.
Sometimes he cries so much that he makes me cry. He's in shock
still. My aunt thinks I'm in shock too and she says I should go to
the doctor. I try and try to imagine what Kevin is feeling but I
can't. I don't know how he can stand it. He doesn't know what
he's going to do in the fall but he's not going back to Hogan and
neither am I, although I don't know what I'm going to do either.

His father comes down here twice a week and takes him to some shrink but I don't think it's doing any good. His father is forever asking him if he wants to go home but he always says no. I'm always very relieved when he says no, like my life depends on it. I bought him a new swimsuit and he's been wearing it ever since.

The sun is at five o'clock, the time of day when if you're facing the water with the sun behind you, beach colors flare and the sky is clear, washed bright blue gray like Kevin's eyes. The tide is flowing out. He just moved the green striped orange umbrella from dry to wet sand nearer the receding surf where the latest shell wreck has just touched down, where every now and then a limp wave will make a last-gasp lame effort to reach his legs. Clouds are sailing in an arc down the sky and up the shore a trawler is headed north, toward the mouth of the Hudson I guess, to Manhattan maybe.

Ⓟ Plume

NOVELS OF GENIUS AND PASSION

℗ Plume

COMING OF AGE

(0452)

☐ **THE FAMILY OF MAX DESIR, by Robert Ferro.** This is the story of Max Desir, a man whose emotions are painfully divided between his Italian-American family—from which he has been exiled—and his lover Nick, with whom he openly takes up life amid the enchantments of Rome and, later, amid the realities of New York.
(255872—$6.95)

☐ **A SMILE IN HIS LIFETIME, by Joseph Hansen.** Whit Miller was gay and now there was nothing to repress who he was and what he wanted: a man to love, among so many men to love. In an odyssey of desperate need and obsessive desire he journeys to the heights and to the depths of the heart—and of the flesh . . .
(256755—$6.95)

☐ **A BOY'S OWN STORY, by Edmund White.** A bittersweet novel of gay adolescence, it has a universality that evokes memories for everyone, male and female, gay and straight: the perplexing rites of passage, the comic sexual experiments, the first broken heart, the thrill of forbidden longing, and the inevitable coming of age.
(254302—$5.95)

☐ **THE BOYS ON THE ROCK, by John Fox.** Sixteen-year-old Billy Connors feels lost—he's handsome, popular, and a star member of the swim team, but his secret fantasies about men have him confused and worried—until he meets Al, a twenty-year-old aspiring politician who initiates him into a new world of love and passion. Combining uncanny precision and wild humor, this is a rare and powerful first novel.
(257530—$6.95)

Prices slightly higher in Canada.

To order use coupon on next page.

PLUME

27 million Americans can't read a bedtime story to a child.

It's because 27 million adults in this country simply can't read.

Functional illiteracy has reached one out of five Americans. It robs them of even the simplest of human pleasures, like reading a fairy tale to a child.

You can change all this by joining the fight against illiteracy.

Call the Coalition for Literacy at toll-free **1-800-228-8813** and volunteer.

Volunteer Against Illiteracy.
The only degree you need is a degree of caring.